BOOKS BY EDWARD LE COMTE

NOVELS

The Professor and the Coed

The Man Who Was Afraid

He and She

CRITICISM AND MISCELLANY

A Dictionary of Puns in Milton's English Poetry

Milton and Sex

Poets' Riddles: Essays in Seventeenth-Century Explication

Milton's Unchanging Mind

The Notorious Lady Essex

Grace to a Witty Sinner: A Life of Donne

A Milton Dictionary

The Long Road Back

Dictionary of Last Words

Yet Once More: Verbal and Psychological Pattern in Milton

Endymion in England: The Literary History of a Greek Myth

AS EDITOR

Paradise Lost and Other Poems

Justa Edovardo King

I, EVE

I, EVE

A Novel by

EDWARD LE COMTE

Atheneum

NEW YORK   1988

Atheneum
Macmillan Publishing Company
866 Third Avenue, New York, N.Y. 10022
Collier Macmillan Canada, Inc.

Library of Congress Cataloging-in-Publication Data
Le Comte, Edward, 1916–
I. Eve : a novel / by Edward Le Comte.
p. cm.
ISBN 0-689-11981-X
1. Eve (Biblical figure)—Fiction. I. Title.
PS3562.E28I14   1988   88-15320
813'.54—dc   CIP

Design by Janet Tingey

Illustrations by Mia Le Comte

10 9 8 7 6 5 4 3 2 1

PRINTED IN THE UNITED STATES OF AMERICA

To Mia, who educated me

ONE

I s this the promised end? He withered away like a cricket. It was hard to believe that he would begin to smell, but I knew what I had to do. I dragged him—how light he was!—down to the stream and packed mud on him. His legs were sticks. All over he was as dry as the shed skin of a snake, shrunken and dry, his head a white bush, the eyes black pebbles—and no blood. The sheepskin slipped aside from his loins. He was dry there too, dry and white.

So different from that other time, so long ago. My son poured out God's plenty of blood, from inside his mouth and from his head. I guess when you're young and strong is when you have it most. Red hyacinth sprung up in the field where he fell. It had been purple before, and so I knew it came from his blood, the new color. The buds reminded me of his curls, which even the rain didn't straighten. I twirled them until Adam said I had to stop, that the boy was getting too old for that.

Adam, of course, said I was wrong about the flower, which he said was a new one that he called spring heath. As if I couldn't recognize a red hyacinth when I saw one! Men don't know flowers. All they know is words. Words, words, words.

He's not going to tell me anymore my name means serpent. Ever since what he was pleased to call my Fall he threw that at me. Oh it seemed like hundreds of years that I had to hear it. "Serpent to serpent," he would shout. "You were fit mates, fitted mates, under that tree."

"And what about that Lilith?" I replied, giving it back to him. "Your demon mistress! The mother of Cain."

It was run or be struck when I put that to him. *"You're* the mother of Cain," he insisted with that high voice that is used for lying. "You would be."

"You tricked me, both of you." We fought that battle a thousand times and then shuddered to silence in each other's arms, as the tiger glared outside our nightly fire and the wolves howled in the hills.

The mouth that I used to stop with kisses I now stopped with mud, it being slightly open. It had dropped open during the darkness, maybe so the soul could get out. Nothing else came from it, no sound, as I sometimes sat and sometimes lay beside him, the whole night, and knew the end was near. He had crossed his arms as if hugging himself. You live together but you die alone, I see that. Who will cover me when my near time comes?

Abel had heaved out his soul with much noise, a wail, an eruption from his chest like an elephant's call, a gurgling of fluids. I heard the whole sequence in my bower. I didn't get there in time to see it. Cain had already run away.

The stream was not full as in the spring: I remember a particular spring, bright with emerging flowers, when Adam and I spoke of death and wondered what it would be like to be under that water and stay under. Somebody else—if there *were* somebody else—would look down and see us lying side by side, a still married couple. Or a married couple still. Now the stream had retreated to its basic bed, deep enough to come up to my waist, leaving plenty of mud behind. In the early morning the air was nipping, like a small animal at my heels. It was the season I call autumn, but which Adam sometimes called fall. That is a word I did not under any circumstances like to hear. "Why have two words that mean the same thing, or worse, one word that means two things?" I objected. "First there was sin, then there was synonym." His eyes wandered off before he answered. I knew he was about to have one of his fits of prophecy. Finally he uttered, without my, or any, lightness, "There will be syntax."

Adam and I had discussed what the one who survived would do with the body of the other. "Maybe we'll meet the end together," I said. "In an accident."

"What accident," he asked, "even supposing there *are*

accidents? A fall"—that word again—"from a cliff? How long has it been since we climbed a cliff? We avoid the deep water. We know what to eat and what not to eat. The beasts, no matter how much they bluster, don't, as you know, like us. They keep their distance as if we stank. We're not strong enough or careless enough to have an accident. That's for the young. No, it will be a natural death. A gentle wafting."

"We could be struck by lightning." (Thunder and lightning terrified me. In my younger days I'd looked out from a convenient cave and seen a hippopotamus bolted down a bank, his little feet raised vainly to heaven.)

"I'm not given to see who will be the first, but it will surely be death from feebleness, the same feebleness that makes it so hard now, even with your hand in mine, to reach the second field."

The second field was where my son had been slain. On that occasion we had merely thrown straw over the twisted body and turned our backs fast. We shouldn't have been surprised—but we were—that overnight it became meat for the fowls of the air and the beasts of the earth. We'd seen it happen to dead animals, but distraught, we failed to draw what Adam afterwards called the obvious conclusion.

Nine hundred years later (that's what it felt like) we weren't about to make the same mistake.

Little Abel had had a pet squirrel that we shoved into a gopher hole, scraping earth with a stick to close it up.

But to make or find something deep enough for a human body and have proper earth to cover it (even with evergreen branches as a base) would be far beyond the means of one weak pair of hands, and so we agreed on mud. Wet mud always felt good to my skin, even salutary. I wouldn't mind it on me, living or dead, in hopes of keeping my body from being violated until it was such as no creature would bother.

Only, unless Seth returns, there will be nobody to put it on me.

Making it stick to his hair wasn't easy. I had to lay it on thick, wet, and heavy, sloshing about as I scooped up the globs and slapped his head with them. The stuff was all over my arms and dugs. What mud fights we had had when we were young, all four of us hurling it, harmlessly except when it got in the eye. Then a naked boy was sure to cry, and I had to show him another thing water was good for.

I saved his face from the birds and myself from his black stare. He had looked as if he were reproaching me for not having been the first to go. Husband, I follow soon. The back of my claw hand is a mate to yours. I don't seek out the reflection of my face anymore. I just watched the years loosen the skin of my hand. I used to be able to draw the skin tight by touching my thumb to my little finger. That was when —forty years ago? I delighted in the color of violets until my veins rose in ugly knots and matched it. (Violets are blue and so are you.)

"You couldn't have lived so long with Lilith," I said. "She'd have killed you. It's monogamy that's kept us alive."

"It's monotony," he answered.

Monogamy and monotony have always been sore subjects. Were we in any danger of monotony before we were driven out of the Mount? The Serpent said we were. Clever, confusing, he said, "It is not immortality if you are bored to death. Try this for variety. It will give you a real high."

His knobby knees took the mud well. My knees were prettier: he always admitted that. They are dimpled, he said. How do dimples differ from wrinkles? Wrinkles are dimples run wild.

Centuries could not dry up the memory of how it once was. You never enjoy the world aright till the sea itself flows in your veins, till you are clothed with the heavens and crowned with the stars and feel yourself to be sole heir of the whole world. That was how it was, the first hour of my creation, when I woke up alone and felt my body and went to a lake's reflection.

Birds were the first sound I heard. Then the purling sound of water drew me. The lake issued from a cave. There were yellow flowers on the bank. I lay down to look into the clear smooth lake that seemed to me another sky. What I saw I did not know was I, but it took my breath away with its beauty. It had tresses like mine. I reached out to touch. It did the same. I started back; it started back. Pleased I soon returned; pleased it returned as soon with answering looks of sympathy and love. I pined with vain desire. I longed to embrace it.

A voice saved me, possibly, from falling in. "Self-love," it said, "that is all very well. But here I am."

He was tall, dark, and handsome. No beard. His eyes and shoulder-length hair were black. I did not know my eyes were blue but the hair that caressed my hips with each step I took towards him was as agreeably brown as the fawn that watched our meeting two unfrightened yards away. The fawn had a perky tail. Adam had one too, but it was in front. His chest was flat.

"Daughter of God and Man, Immortal Eve," he said, when I halted at arm's length.

"Daughter of man?"

"You have just been brought into being from my rib."

That was the Age of Faith. We lay down on a bed of roses—they had no thorns then—and began to do what came naturally. Explanations, detail, he gave me later.

Why, in the first place, his rib? God, the Voice that talked to him but never to me, said, "I will not create her from your head, lest she be light-headed; nor from your eye, lest she be a coquette; nor from the ear, lest she be an eavesdropper;" (that was the first pun!) "nor from your mouth, lest she be a gossip; nor from the hand, lest she be light-fingered; nor from the foot, lest she be a gadabout. I will take her from a place over your heart, so that you may love her and she you forever."

Is there any lovemaking like the first? It was inner and outer paradise both. He was in perfect blissgiving, blissreceiving control of that penis of his. (Afterwards it would control *him*.) We made love all afternoon. He made love to my mouth, to my breasts, to my limbs. He made total love. He saturated every inch of my body with it. We cried in mutual ecstasy dozens of times, oblivious of the flora and fauna of the idyllic setting. We slept through the night, not even being aware that it had arrived, in each other's arms. That is the test of love, too: to hold each other like little children and sleep dreamlessly for twelve hours.

He had the manliness of a man in his giving and the innocence of a child in his pleased receiving. When we woke up he told me how he had asked God for me. He had been alone for three days and had named and gamboled with the animals. The lion lay down with the lamb, and so did he.

He pointed out a leopardess that had been his particular favorite. Her breath was fragrant with strawberries. "Male and female created He them, and the female will bear little ones inside her. And so will you. But they don't make love face-to-face the way we do." Adam had talked to the animals; they answered back with purrs and playful yelps. "I wondered what was the use of me having words if I never got words back. Also they never smile the way you do."

He called out to the Voice. "It is not good that I should be alone. I should have a helpmate."

The Voice answered, "How can you complain of solitude? Is not the earth with various living creatures replenished, and the air, and all these at your command come and play before you? Your kingdom, your paradise, is large."

"The brutes don't talk. They are not my equals. They mate, but I am just a species unto myself, barren, single."

Like a sigh of the wind came the answer, "I have been alone from all eternity."

"With all submission, and begging your pardon, you have good reasons for being a bachelor. But paradise will not be complete for me without a mate, with whom I participate in all rational delight. You made creatures yourself, I believe, in order to love them."

"Thus far to try you, Adam, I was pleased. Your request makes sense, though I hope your senses will not grow wild, too wild, over one bearing some resemblance to you—and possibly even to me—that I will shape from your rib."

My Adam was always queasy about operations, the blood and all. When Abel was being born he did not attend me. He fled into the wood at my groans. The same for Seth. I had to sever the cord myself with my teeth and clean up the mess. Only when the infant stopped crying because it was at my breast did Adam come back for a look.

God was a kindly obstetrician to Adam, putting him into a deep sleep. Adam saw as in a dream—but did not feel—my shaping. "Men are cowards when it comes to pain," I said to him once. "No," he argued, "God's real reason was to spare me repulsion at the shaping process. You recall that egg I opened that was half bird, a slimy black mess."

We didn't say things like that until after the Fall. After the Fall I told him I was tired of his rib story and didn't believe it.

But I'm not forgetting how happy we were till we weren't. Tangled in flowers I fell on grass, just for fun, and Adam joined me. Ripe fruit dropped about my head. I felt my first orange, knew there was good inside. We ate and drank of gourds and watermelons. We picked eleven kinds of berries. Our lips became all colors. We ate hazelnuts, beechnuts, sweet chestnuts. We sipped on honeysuckle. Adam proffered a posy, which I nibbled and found good, buds and stalks: broccoli. There were pears and peaches. Nothing rotted, ever.

We splashed in the Lake of Me. I pointed out that I really was better-looking but that he was perfect. We even made love in water (which later became impossible). We made love anytime we felt like it, which was often, and that became impossible also.

I saw wisps of animals in the clouds. When the greater light set, I was not afraid. I loved the lesser light in its round fullness because I could stare at it as much as I wished. The stars were fire-folk. The trees loomed protectively, some of them as high as the sky. My bed was the savanna and my husband's arms. The birds sang us to sleep, after the monkeys stopped chattering.

Yes, I even enjoyed the monkeys in those days, those masturbating distortions of human beings. There was a douroucouli that leapt from cedar to cedar and spoke to me tenderly with his large soulful brown eyes.

I knew I had a soul. I asked Adam if the animals did.

"No. Only we can be damned."

"Damned? We are immortal. We stay here forever."

"That depends. Of every tree in this garden we may freely eat—except one. One is forbidden: the tree of the knowledge of good and evil, the one with the yellow apples. We may eat of the tree with red apples. But if we eat of the tree with yellow apples, we will become mortal and will have to leave this seat of bliss. We will be exiled and we will know death."

It wasn't a very long speech as speeches later went, but it was the longest up till then. Normally I didn't need explanations and we were in agreement, with few words. It sufficed to exchange "yes" or "I love you" or "I love it."

"Why doesn't the Voice ever speak to me?"

"It's hierarchy. From Him to me. From me to you."

"Is it the yellow that is bad? The moon is yellow. Your leopardess is yellow. Squash is yellow. Jonquils are yellow."

"So is urine," he laughed.

"It's God-given, it's natural. I'd drink it if He told me to."

"You say the right thing. You are obedient. It should be easy to refrain from the yellow apple."

"It seems strange there should be one exception in all that is freely given."

"Eve, sole part and sole partner of all these joys, we have free will: we freely choose. Having free will we must have something to exercise it on, something important, not something trivial like deciding what to have for lunch. So the tree with yellow apples is planted there as offering us a major decision."

"But suppose I wanted a yellow apple for lunch? And I get confused when you combine 'free' with 'must.' "

He took my arm and kissed it. "We have the red. Probably the yellow would taste awful. Why would we want the one thing we are told we mustn't have? Told for our own good. We don't eat bark. We don't eat beetles. We don't eat field mice."

"I wouldn't want a mouse moving in my insides."

That's how ignorant I was of death in those days, those salad days, when I was green in judgment.

My first night was, as I have said, dreamless, blissfully so. It was the next day that Adam told me of the forbidden tree. That night I had my first dream. It was real while it lasted. All my dreams are real while they last, especially my nightmares. This first one wasn't a nightmare. It was exceedingly pleasant. That was the trouble with it.

I was seeing the forbidden tree for the first time, in vivid color. A man leaned against the trunk, his legs crossed. I didn't make out his face clearly but I took the figure to be Adam. What other man could it be? The only difference was he had wings, black like his hair: they seemed a natural extension of his hair and shoulder blades, even as I had been, as the story goes, some sort of outgrowth of his rib. When he saw that I saw him he walked towards me and his wings opened and closed slowly like a big black butterfly posed on a sunflower. His left hand proffered me a yellow apple. "Here, happy creature," he intoned, "fair angelic Eve, partake. Fly with me: not to earth confined. Ascend to heaven." He brushed my lips with the apple. The pleasant savory smell so quickened appetite that I could not but taste. Forthwith up to the clouds with him I flew and underneath beheld the earth outstretched, with the four rivers winding out of Eden. Then I awoke.

Adam was leaning on his elbow, watching me.

"I just had another life," I said.

"What you had was a dream. It wasn't real. You were flushed and disturbed."

"It was real. How do we know *we* are real?"

"There are different theories. One is that we are such stuff as dreams are made on and our little life—if it *were* a little life—is rounded with a sleep. That would mean we are God's dream."

"And when He wakes up?"

"We are no more. But remember, we are to be forever. That is the difference between life and dreaming. Duration. Your dream, I daresay, was just a few moments. Tell me it."

My recital made him frown. "I cannot like this uncouth dream. I shouldn't have told you about the forbidden tree. But I had to tell you. Now you've got it too much on your mind. Evil into the mind of God or man may come and go, and leave no spot behind, but still . . . Sin can occur even before the act. It can occur with the consent. Did you consent?"

"I told you I took a bite. It was pressed on me, by you."

"It wasn't me."

"My author and disposer, the only dream you ever had was of me. And it was real."

"That wasn't a dream. That was a vision, a true vision."

"In any case I sinned only—and I must say it was all very pleasant—in a dream. Can I be blamed for that?"

"There's a theory that dreams represent hidden wishes."

"I *would* like to fly."

"There is one other thing I have to warn you about. We should have this Mount all to ourselves. But I have intimations there is at least one other person lurking about. He is an outsider: he doesn't belong here. He envies us our happiness. He will spoil it if he can. Watch out. Stay by my side."

I embraced him tightly. "O you for whom and from whom I was formed flesh of your flesh, why would I ever want to leave your side, whence I came?"

After oranges and tomatoes and grapes we got up to do our light gardening. It consisted of pulling away matted vines and clearing undergrowth and pruning fruit trees large and small. It helped pass the day, as did hugs and kisses. When we felt the sun at noon we bathed in the Euphrates, by the side of which we picked up pretty red and green stones. We made love standing in the water and lying on the bank. He placed a garland of daisies on my head. Then he stuck violets in my lower hair. "Your mount, my beloved, is a microcosm of *the* Mount," he fancily said.

"Why all the lushness?" I inquired on that third afternoon of my life. "Why is there so much of everything? Is it to give us something to do?"

"It won't be too much when the children come," he answered, "and the children's children."

Beyond the fields there were no paths except those we forced with our feet and hands. In the forest I began to feel hemmed in. I looked up at the monkeys that moved so easily among the trees, while Adam and I barely inched our way. Our feet were tortoise-slow. All other animals moved faster. A squirrel could scramble up a tall oak and disappear in a moment. There were even squirrels that had wings: they *flew* from tree to tree.

I had no particular longing for a yellow apple. The red were fine. But the more I lifted my head and watched the birds, the more I wanted to fly. I envied the falcon its graceful swoop, the swallow its lightness on a branch. Butterflies were free in a way I wasn't. I felt heavy, earthbound. My four-footed friends outran me. I could not catch up with a gazelle or a cheetah unless it chose to stop teasing and stood in its tracks for one stroke of its flank and a kiss on the muzzle.

And I *had* flown: that was the unforgettable thing. My undreaming husband could not comprehend what it was like to be up in the blue, looking down on the whole earth, soaring over the tallest trees, transcending the littleness of our petty, grass-entangled pace and blocked vision. For unspeakable seconds I had God's view. My flight-companion had called me "angelic," with some appropriateness since angels have wings—as he had, black and powerful, powerful enough for two.

The fourth day of my life I woke with the dawn. A thousand birds twittered and screeched, and some animal grunted. My sleep had been blank again, to my disappointment. It didn't look as if the sweet dream of flight would ever return.

Adam lay sleeping on his side, facing me, but his arms had slipped from me. We didn't even have a bower in those days. We just slept in the grass. The bugs didn't crawl on us. I had yet to see rain. It was dry spring, or perhaps early summer.

Easy it would be, easy it was, for me to get up and explore the nearby forest. I had some time to myself, as when I first woke up to life, and the birds, then also, were the first sound to greet me. I hadn't longed for Adam in those moments: I didn't know he existed. I was busy discovering myself when he called after me.

I'd be back before he stirred, with berries for him, maybe some fruit we hadn't yet tried. I got the impression we could find something new to eat every day in all that dew-laden abundance. I went by colors. Brown never attracted me. Not that I didn't like my own hair, which I sometimes put into my mouth.

A turn in the wood here, another turn there, and I came upon a clearance with one conspicuous tree. A man was stretched out at the foot of it, his head propped against it. He had short yellow hair. His penis was covered by a coiled snake. He fondled its neck—if a snake can be said to have a neck. In my opinion a snake is all neck. I didn't cotton to snakes. I certainly wouldn't make a pet of one as this newcomer had done. They seemed slimy. In fact I would say, in the light of my whole experience, that the fork-tongued serpent is more subtile than any beast of the field which the Lord

God has made. Give me an innocent lamb or a hare any day. (Soon I would cook both.)

The tree was the one with yellow apples. I had passed it the morning after I had dreamed of it. There was no point, I gathered, in its being hidden or hard to find if we were to exercise our free will on it. The stranger held in his left hand a product of the tree from which a bite had been taken, either by him or his scaly friend. After staring up at me with his pale blue eyes—his body was much hairier than Adam's—he lowered his head, perhaps in an effort to conceal (my eyes were sharp in those days) some tremor in his lips while the serpent was speaking. I myself trembled in my whole body at words from a brute.

The voice and sentiments were male. "Empress of this fair world, resplendent Eve, O wonder, O wounder of hearts, my lovely fair, where is your angel train, where are your wings?"

"I wish I had them. But who gave you speech?"

The blond stranger looked up and smiled before lowering his head again.

"I was at first as other beasts that graze the trodden herb, of abject thoughts and low, as was my food—until I tasted the apple."

"The fruit of that tree?"

"Precisely."

"We are forbidden the yellow apples."

"Who forbade you?"

"My creator."

He half uncoiled himself as if to illustrate his next words. "Your creator was somebody's penis, and pricks don't talk."

I turned to go. I didn't care for his untrue words at all. It was the first lie I had ever heard and I wanted it to be the last.

"Do not go," he wheedled. "You said you wanted wings. I can give them. But don't flee the facts either. Who do *you* think was your creator? "

"The fruit may have given you words but not sense. I came from Adam's rib."

"So Adam was your creator?"

"The material came from him but the shaping was by another hand."

"Do you remember your creation?"

"No, but my husband does."

The snake flicked his black tongue and let out air like a hiss, then settled down on the man's lap again. "If you don't remember, you don't know. You didn't see it. You just have Adam's word for it. Have you ever met this so-called creator?"

"The messages come from Adam, who hears them."

"A likely story! He just wants to keep you down, in subjection, dependent. And, speaking of dependency, what do you think that charming dent in the middle of your belly means? It's not just for holding peanuts. You came squalling into the world with an umbilical cord.

You were born of woman and made by man. You're big enough to be told."

"I'm four days old and I don't believe you ate of the yellow apple. If you did you'd be dead. God hath said, 'Ye shall not eat of it, neither shall ye touch it, lest ye die.' "

The stranger took another bite out of the apple, then threw it away. Next with both hands he gathered up the serpent and hurled it towards a bush, where it slithered out of sight.

"Enough of this nonsense," he said, getting up. He plucked another apple from the tree. It was interesting how it matched his hair. "I touch. I eat. How alive, how potent, I am, you will shortly see. I yield to none when it comes to flattery, but lady, you will grow old and die no matter what you do or don't. The snake renews its skin, but you aren't even capable of that."

I was unused to and weary of argument. I was also hungry. "Who are you?" I demanded.

"Call me Nonbeliever. I disbelieve in everything except freedom. I can liberate you. I can make you as free as a vulture. This apple will give you flight."

He proffered it, as had been done in my dream.

I was by now extremely hungry. Had there been a date tree or something else nearby I'd have gone to it for breakfast. But the Tree of the Knowledge of Good and Evil stood all by itself, with nothing edible nearby. I suppose, again, that that was to make the choice definite.

"If I eat that I will surely die."

"You will surely die in any case."

"I do not know what death is except that it is terrible. I have not seen it."

"Just wait. You can't expect many corpses in four days. What do you do with time anyway?"

"We make love and we garden."

"I will be a second lover to you, and as for immortality, it is not immortality if you are bored to death. Try this for variety. It will give you a real high."

It smelled good, now almost brushing my nostrils. Would it kill me if it touched me rather than I it? That would not be fair. I repeated with all my remaining strength, "I must not eat of the yellow apple. I must not. I must not."

I was so weak I sat down on the sward. Why was Adam still sleeping, if he was? Maybe he would come if I cried out. Maybe this was another dream. I should scream myself awake. But no, my voice stuck in my throat. I could not even get out another "I must not." I made furry sounds like an animal.

"I tell you what, fair lady," said the tempter, blessedly withdrawing his arm. "I'll fix it for you. It's the yellow that's forbidden, isn't it, according to the story your man tells? Yellow fruit, yellow me. It shall cease to be yellow forthwith."

Stooping over, he gathered a flowering herb. He squeezed a juice from the flowers onto the apple, spreading it all around. The apple turned brown.

"This is pure, unadulterated. Thou shalt not commit

adulteration. Resin is choice. I guarantee this is a bhang. Acid is grovy. Or gravy."

The tempter sat down in front of me, his knees spread as mine were, the feet touching. I had seen two chimpanzees in this same posture. I myself had totally lost the power of speech. The apple was again at my mouth. It had a peculiar, sickening, dizzying odor. I was curious whether the taste would be like the smell.

At the same time I did not lose my aversion to brown, which I wanted to mention but was unable to. My empty stomach urged me forward. Why did God give a healthy, innocent woman an appetite if He did not mean for her to satisfy it? Also, as the man said— probably he was as wise as Adam, if not wiser—the fruit being no longer yellow had become a different and unforbidden fruit. Why, indeed, was any fruit forbidden? Did God give only to take away?

Above all (so to speak) I would fly. I would be more than a bird: I would be an angel, even a god, in my soaring, looking down upon the whole earth and the little creatures on it. Even the elephant or the giraffe would look small and Adam would no longer be tall. If he was good—but he would have to be very good, good to me—I might share the magic plant with him. But not right away. I would soar alone, be alone again as in those first superb moments when I had no peer except my own faint image in the water, and no one issued orders.

If I'd been standing I'd have dropped, my sinews loosened. My chin was quivering, which meant that my mouth was half open like dead Adam's. The brown rind was at my teeth.

If only to keep from choking, I bit. Consent? What a cold and calculating word! God knows—I hope He knows—this was no planned and premeditated act. A dream is not premeditation. A wish to fly is a harmless fantasy. Besides, only the self-tempted should be lost forever. Rapture had descended to rape.

In natural process I chewed and swallowed. I gobbled it down, one mouthful, without tasting it. Tasting would have been willful. I was bent on just getting it over with, my fate. You don't savor your fate.

You just suffer the aftereffects, which were that the earth reeled and went blank. I mean my surroundings lost their natural color, their green and brown and yellow. I couldn't look up, but I'm sure the sky was no longer blue. White took over completely in the tempter's pale eyes. His iris and pupil were gone, I was being stared at by two white orbs, egg-white, two moons (how could I have ever liked the moon?) that advanced on me and held me down as surely as if I had been bound in hemp.

The voice was worse. "Beast," he hissed. "Turn over on all fours. Now. Stick up your rear. I will not go where he went."

And he did not go where Adam went and then I first knew pain. I cried and cried unheeded.

Afterwards he stood over me as I wept, his legs straddling me. "Rejoice you've been spared impregnation with a female shit like yourself or a bastard boy. Worm you are and worm you will come to. Create—do you think *I* want to create? What in hell for?"

Then I first knew hatred. It kept echoing long after he had vanished into the forest.

But that devil (who was never seen again, thank God!) spoke some truth. After a time I went from sore to soar. I did fly. It was not so much that I left the earth as that the earth left me. The ground dropped from under my prone body. I looked down into distance, which meant that I was on high. Everything receded, either vertically or horizontally—the no longer brown tree with the no longer yellow apples, the bushes, the clearing. It all became one white cloud, in the midst of which—or in the mist of which—I rocked.

This was unearthly fun. I heard myself giggle. I groped in my cloud until I found the rest of the apple, no longer recognizable by color but by the bite I had taken out of it.

If I was generous—and if I could put one foot in front of the other—this was to be shared. For once I knew something that Adam didn't, a sensation that would make his head reel. Sole part of all my joys, he had said. Partner. Share and share alike.

An animal roared somewhere outside my cloud. I rolled over on my back and endeavored to think. Share what alike? Adam would claim it was death. He was sure to preach. He was always preaching.

Was it death? Was I dead and in heaven? Then he should go with me, flesh of my flesh. Partner.

A voice said, "What are you doing there, Eve, lolling on the ground?"

At first I thought it was *the* Voice, the Voice that had never before spoken to me. I was in heaven and God was welcoming me. Only His tone did not have the warmth I should have expected.

Adam bent down and I held up the apple.

"Take a bite. You'll never feel the same again."

"What is it?"

"It's not yellow. You can see it's brown." (I couldn't.) "Eat and soar."

He looked doubtfully in the direction of the tree. "I never saw a brown apple before. Apples are either red or—yellow. Brown may mean it isn't good. You yourself told me you didn't care for anything brown."

"I've changed my mind. I was wrong."

I have a fairly clear conscience. I did not tell him anything that was not true. I just did not tell him everything. I was to tell him about the snake but never about the devil and what he did to me. That would have changed our relationship irreparably. It would have been better all around if *he* had managed to keep Lilith a secret.

Besides, if he was as smart as he thought he was, he

could have figured everything out. I take no responsibility for what he did of his own free will when I offered him what he in fact got—a new sensation, of wings and clouds and flight.

He ate the apple; indeed he finished it. I told him to lie down beside me for best effect. "It takes some while."

"I see you are exact of taste, babe," he finally commented, after swiveling his head in an odd way. "Babe in the woods. How about a little lovin'? I lust for you, those boobs, your nest of honey, everything." And he began slobbering over me, as if I were dirty and needed a bath. He followed this by nipping my breasts, at first lightly, then so sharply that I cried out and pushed him away.

He rolled back on me and tried to get *it* in but it remained flaccid.

"Are you a man or a mouse's tail," I jeered.

"Damn it, give me time." He tried to masturbate like a monkey, but nothing worked. "Maybe if you sucked it?" he proposed.

I was hot, boy was I hot, but not that hot. I fingered myself. "To hell with you," I shouted, and lay on my stomach where I could do it better.

Next I knew, a boar was chasing me. He wanted to toss me on his curved tusks. He came nearer and nearer with his little red porcine eyes. He had a tusk for each of my breasts.

I sat up in a sweat from my first nightmare. It was still day in the jungle. The bestial sound in my ears was Adam snoring. Furious I shook him. He wasn't going to sleep if I couldn't.

He looked at me as if I were a stranger. "That fallacious fruit. Why did you take it—why did you bring it?"

"The serpent beguiled me, and I did eat."

"You are the serpent that beguiled me. We have lost immortality, the garden, all."

"We never had immortality. Dying is just a question of when. You lied."

I leant over and jabbed his ribs, each of them, and counted out loud. Twelve on the left side. Just so there could be no argument I counted his other side as well. When I came to the last rib I punched it, hard. "You lied so you could order me around. I was to pay Big Daddy endless gratitude and worship, I the rib, you my author and disposer and the sole hearer of divine voices who in fact snorts like a pig and is impotent."

"What an insatiable bitch you are! Try a ram. You don't deserve to know that you came from an extra rib, a thirteenth, which of course is now gone. Would I had kept it! From now on, evil Eve, thirteen will be an unlucky number. And *sinister*, once simply a synonym for *left*, I now declare to be a word of ill omen, thanks to the Fall in which you entangled me. I asked for a helpmate, and got—you."

He was positively spluttering.

I staggered to my feet and straddled him like a conqueror. I felt like raining down urine on his face. "Your limp snake of a penis disgusts me. I never realized before how very ugly it is. Why don't you have the decency to hide it."

"And what do you think you look like as I gaze up you. If you knew, you'd cover yourself with your hands."

I stepped away from him and went further into the woods.

"Yes, leave my side," he shouted after me. "Why did you ever?"

The day before, Adam and I had sheltered in the cool of the biggest tree in the forest. It was a forest in itself. The ends of the branches hung down and touched the ground, where they took root so that even the twigs became trees. It was a fig tree, with broad leaves. Adam did not refrain from a little anatomical joke about figs, whereupon I called it the mother-tree. Its grounded offshoots were its daughters. We played hide-and-seek in the loopholes. The echoes equaled those of caves. Such was the joy when we, girl and boy, in our youth time were seen on the echoing green.

I was busy twining leaves about my waist when Adam turned up. "Good," he said. "I'm glad you took my advice. A little more obedience would have kept us alive. You look a lot better. Fig to fig."

I glanced contemptuously at his dangling snake. "Take *my* advice."

We went our separate ways, with a rustling of skirts.

He called out, not far away. "Eve, Eve, come here quick!"

I took my time. He was in the field gazing down on a fawn that lay on its side without moving. It was the same fawn, I was sure, that witnessed our marriage. Its eye saw nothing. Its bloody ribs were exposed, its side torn away.

"I heard an animal run away when I emerged," he said. "It's begun. They may go after us next."

"Not in Eden," I answered.

"Yes, in Eden."

But that became a moot point because we left Eden in a hurry. The sky darkened with more than the onset of night. When thunder and lightning came with the rain I screamed and began running. I ran down the Mount, and Adam after me. I slipped and slid and tumbled. I was cut and scratched with no leisure to feel it. All I could think of was to flee the vengeance, as the sky crackled and trees split and the forest blazed behind me.

I knew I was out of Eden when I crashed through a thornbush. The storm in the distance subsided, with a flash here and there, and the last growls of an angry deity, but the forest continued burning. I wondered if any animals remained alive. I hoped most of them were gone forever, since I was afraid of them now, but they had been my friends and I tried to imagine what it would be like to be burned alive.

The darkness of night had succeeded, with no moon, no stars. I could not see Adam, but his voice was bitter. "You know, I keep thinking of what a mistake I made in asking God for you. I pleaded for the gift of you. And now I've got you."

"You said that before. I'm not even sure it's true."

"I erred in putting my trust in an outside fair. Or was it the sense of touch that undid me? Those whom the gods wish to punish, they answer their prayers."

"I see you've become a polytheist."

"Would there were some other way to generate mankind, if indeed I want to generate mankind."

"Better see if you can."

"Thorns and thistles it has already brought, but more than all these wounds and bruises it's going to hurt you."

"What?" I was thinking of my first hurt, the one I would never tell him about.

"Childbirth. In sorrow thou shalt bring forth children."

"And you sit back and enjoy it? We could call everything off right now. One more smug word from you and this rib is going to walk away forever."

"Let's not quarrel. I don't mean to quarrel. I was just thinking out loud. I am cursed too—with labor by the sweat of my brow for bread. You make it but I have to toil for the wheat. Nothing's going to drop into our hands anymore."

With the word "hands" he reached out both of his, and I accepted him, now potent again, and we drugged ourselves as best we could with frantic lovemaking.

TWO

"It's the female that bites."

Adam said this of the mosquito. I would say it of Lilith. Both came out of the bushes.

I have no interest in the sex life of the mosquito, except to wish it would cease. Male and female created He them, no doubt, if Adam wasn't making a malicious joke. Flowers strike me as much sexier, with their pistils and their stamens. Take orchids—should I mention what they remind me of? I giggled it into my husband's ear, and he said that that was exactly what their name meant.

There was strife between dryness and dampness, and the mosquito won. So intense was the fire on the Mount that for a night and a day we could feel it. The heat, turning every way, both warmed and warned our bodies, forbidding any fantasy of return. When the fire was at last spent, there was, indeed, nothing to return to. All was black and charred up there.

We moved into a cave and worried about closing it to beasts. But when the bats went out, the mosquitoes whirred in, their whine about as bad as their bite. I was driven to wish I couldn't hear. We slapped at them at night and missed, bruising our fingers. We made bloody blots on our bodies in the daytime. "Maybe we should wear more," Adam suggested. I answered, "We can never cover everything." Sleep was intermittent. A dream couldn't get in edgewise.

Actually they forced us to strike a fire. A fire at the mouth of the cave, we figured, should protect us from all pests, four-footed and flying. "If only the lightning would return and set that maple on fire!" Adam exclaimed. "God, no," I said.

I was idly banging a stone on the floor of the cave. Sparks flew. Adam went out into the sunshine and brought back some dry grass. He pounded. I pounded. We pounded together with two stones. The occasional sparks were as useless as fireflies.

"It has something to do with friction," he observed. "I know it does. We need to rub together what will itself burn."

He invented, clever caveman, what I called the whirlstick. There was a fallen dry tree with a sunken spot in it like a navel. Set there to remind us of our own Fall? Set there to help us? Make of it what you will and Adam did. He took a round dry hardwood stick, held it upright with the lower end in the hole, and turned it rapidly with both hands. The leaves caught fire. And we learned to move our fire where we wanted it, even as we learned to scoop up water for drinking with something less leaky than our hands—the beautiful oval leaves of the rubber plant.

As regards the sweat-of-the-brow curse, food was harder to find. We had to forage. The fruits and vegetables were few and far between. Often there was rot, in whole or in part, or the insects and worms and birds got there first. We wondered how we could add to our intake. I never did make bread, whatever that is. I didn't know how. But our sparse diet needed supplementing.

Animals eating animals disgusted me. The hyena was the worst, except possibly for the vulture. ("Fly like a vulture," the tempter said. Did he also mean eat like one?) The hyena didn't do his own killing: no sweat of the brow there. And he emitted a hideous laugh. Raw flesh offended my nostrils, at its freshest. "But you can see it's eatable," said Adam.

One day he was lugging a sheep away that some animal had partially eaten and had abandoned at our cave entrance. Adam tripped and the carcass fell into the fire. There was no retrieving it and soon we didn't want to because it smelled good. That is how we discovered roast lamb. We also savored hare.

So Adam became a hunter and I a cook. He strangled the sheep and stoned the hare. A young gazelle, fleeing some four-footed predator, got tangled up in liana and Adam despatched it. The meat turned out to be quite solid, yet tender and very sweet. I had never glimpsed these lovely leapers with their flicking tails except at sundown. This specimen tasted of twilight and mimosa blossoms and dew. "It's what they eat that makes them what they are," I commented. "They don't eat twilight," said my uncomprehending husband. "And by your theory we're getting more animalistic."

It was I who discovered how good the marrow of an elk's jawbone was. It was Adam with a flint scraper that he still held in his hand who made a terrifying return as a leopard on hind legs. He had left me saying he had a surprise for me.

"You didn't kill it?"

"Of course not."

"Is that what you do to the thing you loved—the leopardess with the strawberry breath?"

"I tell you the smell was very other. It wasn't the same one." He had secretly dried the pelt. It was certainly an improvement, as it got less warm, over a fig-leaf skirt.

"Let me try it on."

"It's mine, you know. The next is yours."

"You said it was a surprise *for me*. Remember?"

"The surprise was yours. You screamed, didn't you? This skin is mine."

Call that hairsplitting, if you like, ha, ha. I proposed taking turns with it. I ended up wearing it more often, on the grounds that I looked better in it and was more subject to shivers. He eventually got a cheetah, no bad match.

There was no shortage of carcasses lying about, every time we explored. The living animals growled but somehow never attacked, not that I didn't continue to be afraid of the fiercest. They evidently preferred eating each other. Death snarled all around, but it was the dying blossoms that affected me most. They shriveled horribly and I had no way of knowing that they would ever flower again. Would the sturdy oak fall too, as another tree already had? It took years for me to perceive the pattern in the seasons and their small changes. In Eden I knew things intuitively. Now knowledge came hard.

The knowledge that came hardest was that Adam was spending time with another woman.

I wish there had been more guidance from above on marriage. All we had was "Therefore shall a man leave his father and his mother, and shall cleave unto his wife: and they shall be one flesh." The father-and-mother part fitted only Seth and his generation. As for "cleave," Adam suddenly declared, when I was pressing him hard about his infidelity, that it was another of those words with two, in this case even opposite, meanings. He took a piece of flint and split a red apple (the yellow were gone forever) down the middle. " 'Cleave' also means to divide, to separate," he said.

"So God told you to leave me."

"I haven't left you."

You want to have your apple and eat it too, I wittily thought, but didn't say because I was leery of mentioning apples. Instead I retorted, "You may as well leave me." Even in the heat of it all I didn't say leave me. He had two women. He was well off. I had nobody except him, and him less and less. It was grossly unfair. I certainly wasn't longing for that blond fiend. There was speculation of other men somewhere, and other women— perhaps on the other side of the mountain—but I never encountered them.

It was the growing failure to be "one flesh" that finally moved me from innocence to suspicion. What is the proper amount of lovemaking? Heaven was silent. Our lovemaking dwindled. It left us depressed, out of sorts, sulky and sad. In Eden we invariably felt ecstasy together. Now one or the other would turn away unsatisfied. Either I couldn't finish or he couldn't. Increasingly often he couldn't even start. If he did finish once, that was it for days. Advances on my part seemed to embarrass him. I would kiss him, not even expecting anything, and his eyes would look scared and he would pull away. I myself was afraid of having hurled at me again that terrible hurt: "Insatiable." I did everything to improve our bed of branches and flowers. There came the night when he complained his back hurt and he stretched out on the cave floor. There came another night when he didn't return from "hunting" at all.

I have given considerable thought to this problem of togetherness in marriage. How together—in every sense of the word—should a couple be? Adam and I came into the world almost at the same time. Did the rib story really mean that I should never leave his side? Was I punished for leaving his side?

Should we be together absolutely all the time? Is that what love is? Should the one stand by while the other evacuated? Once you grant a tiny separation, all other separations are but ones of degree. Should he leave me behind to hunt while I prepared the food we already had? Or should I hunt with him and he cook with me? When we walked, should we always hold hands? Did having a chance to miss each other strengthen our union?

Into any space between us may any other person come? Emphatically not Lilith, being what she was and doing what they did together. I wouldn't give that demon a piece of lettuce. I never handed her my husband.

Time doesn't dim the memory of that first night he didn't return. I kept the home fires burning. The fire and the smoke helped immensely against the mosquitoes and fended off the beasts of the earth that since Eden I never trusted. Had one turned on Adam? Had he fallen in climbing for a fruit and was lying disabled? Had he got lost in the forest? We had always been careful to limit our exploration, not to lose light and direction.

My first impulse was to go look for him. I stood outside and peered. I called again and again, getting mocking sounds in return. The monkeys and one cawing bird were particularly amused. My further thought was that it would do no good if both of us got lost in that darkness. He should see the fire, and when he got home he should see me.

Two sweet potatoes were lying side by side in the ashes. With two bamboo sticks I picked one up and started munching it—more food than an apple because there was no core. (I hadn't yet learned the purpose of seeds.) Even with this warm delicacy in hand and stomach, a shiver overtook me. He had never missed a meal before, not even the midday one. Was he dead? Was he carrion?

I lay awake on our bed till break of day, staring at the fire and darkness beyond and finally the gathering light. A form darkened the cave entrance. It was Adam, and the first thing I noticed was that he was empty-handed.

I was glad to have him back but was determined not to say so. He sat down beside me. A hug and a kiss from my husband would have been appropriate, I rather thought, but they were not forthcoming. As for me, I was not going to display insatiableness, no matter how much I wanted his arms.

Since he volunteered nothing, I asked, "What happened?"

"It grew dark and I couldn't find my way out, so I slept there."

No human being could sleep in the jungle because of the mosquitoes and the red ants.

"Why didn't you leave while it was still day?"

"I was too far in."

He was too far in, all right. He was too far into her, as I would discover. Liars sooner or later make unintentional puns, as if the truth will out, one way or another.

It was hard to connect with his evasive eyes and show my incredulity.

"You must have brought home much food."

He got up, stooping the way we had to. "No luck. Better luck today, maybe. I'll go now."

"There's a sweet potato out there."

"I've eaten. See you at noon."

I scrambled up and watched from the mouth of the cave the direction he took.

But I didn't stalk him then. I watched and waited. He was certainly up to something. Perhaps he had a cache of food that he didn't want to share.

Four nights later he stayed out all night again. I arose once to throw wood on the fire, but otherwise I slept soundly. He would get no more worry from me. Nor did I ask questions when he returned, even later than before. Why should I elicit pitiful lies? It was beneath my dignity. Why should I care? And he maintained silence, a silence that bristled between us. In the clear light of day, love was not in his looks but apparent guilt, a sad comedown for a man who professed so much piety, who claimed to have had long conversations with God but did not greet his wife.

It is a sad truth, too, that those who have wronged you are angry with you for that very reason. In bed the question of his impotence ceased to arise, because he turned his back on me. He complained about the food that I, not he, had gone out and found.

"Something should be done with these beans."

"I could throw them in your face."

One morning he sneaked out of the cave early, imagining I was asleep. This time I stalked him. I waited till he disappeared into the first clump of trees on the east, then ran quietly after. He wouldn't be expecting me and once I was out of the open space and in the forest noisy with awakening life I was neither seen nor heard. My head was a whirl of flying pests. I couldn't risk slapping. Only hunger ever drove us into the forest.

I shortly discovered, to my shock, what his appetite was, what it was for. He walked at a leisurely pace by about eight trees, perhaps counting (from tree to tree will journey be), turned to the left, and there she was. Before he turned he pushed back his hair and adjusted his cheetah skin.

Evidently convenience is an important factor in affairs. No use having far to go. We tire easily. She should be near, readily available, or why bother? Men are fundamentally lazy. They don't do all for love. They do the minimum. This too infuriated me. I'd seen him go four times as far for a dead boar.

They didn't say a word. They were too hungry for that. From my shelter of bracken I saw a tall slender white form—she was taller and thinner than I and shamelessly naked, no fig leaves, nothing. Both standing, they embraced and kissed with loud suction. She was blonde, as my seducer had been. I couldn't detect the color of her eyes, because they were fervently closed. One hand around his shoulder, her other was loosening his spotted coat, which dropped off. Shoulder and bare buttock were now swayed groundward, and as they toppled I fled.

There are things you just don't look on at, under any circumstances.

When he sauntered home for the noon meal, his garment back on, I was sorely tempted to ask questions for the bitter amusement of seeing what story he would make up. But is not the person who solicits a lie the coauthor of it? God knows, there had been sinning enough already.

Instead I inquired, "Doesn't she feed you?"

He was sucking the marrow of a bone, which he reluctantly took from his mouth. "What did you say?"

Maybe, so noisily absorbed, he really hadn't heard me. "I said, doesn't *she* feed you, the one with the small breasts?"

He set the deer bone down, beside the fire. "So you

know. You've seen her. I knew you would come to know, sooner or later."

"It's been later rather than sooner. You've been going to her for a long while. Spending yourself till you had nothing for me, me the insatiable!"

The grievous thing about being unanswerable is that you do hope for an answer but don't receive one. He told me, as if I cared, "Her name is Lilith. She comes from the other side of the mountain."

"And when is she going back?"

He seized my arm before I could escape. "Eve darling, you're my one and only wife. I love you as I cannot love anyone else."

"I find it hard to remember. What does she do for you?"

"She gives me pleasure. I have to admit that. It's wild. It would be wicked if it were serious—but it's only play, like playing with that leopardess. She is like a feline, all instinct, sensual. Except that I have never seen her eat."

"So you couple on the moss. What about the mosquitoes? They don't pierce your ecstasy?"

"It's a funny thing, it's a very funny thing. When I'm with her the mosquitoes don't come near. She goes completely naked all the time and she is never bothered. I'm bothered only to and fro, never with her."

"So even the mosquitoes won't have her. Only you."

"Meet her. It's right that you should meet her."

"You, of course, are the great authority on Right and Wrong. As handed down from on high. It had not been right, apparently, that you should inform me of her, but now that I've found out, she's to move in, is she? To save you a few steps. Tell me, lord and master— while I hold my breath—is you having two women right? If I may still be described as being had. I don't see it among the animals."

I stood looking down at him across the fire and really did hold my breath.

"I don't know. I can't help it."

"When I told you I couldn't help eating the brown apple I didn't receive the sympathy you now expect from me."

"You know what that brought on us."

"And what will she bring on us?"

"Nothing. That's why I want you to know her. See for yourself that she is harmless. I want you to be friends."

"Cozy."

He jumped up and there was nothing I could do to prevent him from hallooing towards the woods, "Kalee, Kalee!" It was a wild animal cry. I never suspected it meant anything. Later I learned it was his pet name for her and meant, he said, beautiful. He had no pet name for me. I wasn't his pet and doubted that I wanted to be. Pets are animals.

What were my choices? I could retreat into the cave, only to be followed. Walking away wouldn't free me from them and I couldn't relish having my back stared at as they made mocking comments behind it. Running would be loss of dignity and equally futile. I had no choices. Men are physically stronger and work their way.

The woods turned strangely silent as the white figure emerged. No birds sang. Her hair was long, her foot was light, and her eyes were wild. They were set on an almond slant and were leopard green. I wouldn't have minded a truly bright green, like vegetation in full health, but the paleness of her eyes gave the impression of diminished life and function. It was as if they were turned inward rather than outward. It was as if she could barely see. I remembered—how could I forget? —how the blond devil had gone completely blank. Maybe she was meant for the dark. The sun did her no favor. She wouldn't have retained that whiteness if she spent time in it. Adam and I were, long since, as brown as the bark of a crab apple tree.

She, a head taller, his size, came up all too close. It would be some time before I would be in a position to characterize her voice as boyish, light, not an instrument for serious discourse. In her arrogance she didn't bother to give volume, breath. She made one strain to hear, as if for a whisper, which gave her the advantage of causing one to act as if her words were important, of cocking an ear for them.

"So you're the woman of property," she murmured.

"What do you insinuate?"

"In sin you ate," she mocked. "How clever you are! What a long word! Better broken up for its true meaning, yes? Eve, wifely Eve, what I insinuate is that you think you own, have exclusive rights to, this man. The word of the future—an ugly short one—is slave."

"On the contrary, I slave and you enjoy."

"We can all enjoy." Her hand snaked its way through my hair to the nape of my neck, which she commenced to caress up and down with feathery light fingers. Her other hand pushed at my breast. Had she sought to bare it from the leopard covering, I would of course have resisted. But she was subtle, subtler than any beast of the field. It was the leopard skin she rubbed, spreading sensation—as her bare hand on one bare spot never could have—across my whole bosom. Her pale eyes held mine as she maintained a slow rubbing rhythm front and back. "Paradise is not lost," she hissed.

"I don't know about that," said my husband, coming up and taking her hands away for reasons best known to himself.

She turned to him, her hands now being held by him.

"Shall we dance?" she asked. "Sing and dance?"

"What is that?"

Disengaging, she clapped her hands over her head, swayed her white hips, her hair kissing her body in rhythm, and danced sinuously around us and between us, slowly, as if she wanted us to learn the steps. And she sang in a high voice words that were the easier to remember because some of them made melody with others.

There is sweet music here that softer falls
Than petals from blown roses on the grass,
Or night-dews on still waters between walls
Of shadowy granite, in a gleaming pass;
Music that gentlier on the spirit lies,
Than tired eyelids upon tired eyes;
Music that brings sweet sleep down from the blissful skies.
Here are cool mosses deep,
And through the moss the ivies creep,
And in the stream the long-leaved flowers weep,
And from the craggy ledge the poppy hangs in sleep.

She dropped her hands to her sides and stopped in front of me. I was thinking that my breasts were too large for such a nude lewd dance.

"Poor Eve," she cooed. "You look as if you don't sleep well."

Then, without dance, she addressed a song to me.

Why are we weighed upon with heaviness,
And utterly consumed with sharp distress,
While all things else have rest from weariness?
All things have rest: why should we toil alone,

We only toil, who are the first of things,
And make perpetual moan,
Still from one sorrow to another thrown:
Nor ever fold our wings,
And cease from wanderings,
Nor steep our brows in slumber's holy balm;
Nor harken what the inner spirit sings,
"There is no joy but calm!"
Why should we only toil, the roof and crown of things?

"I wish I had wings to fold," I said. I never meant to talk to her, but she had her charm, she beguiled me and made it hard to hate her.

"In a manner of speaking we can fly," she answered.

"Let's not get into that again," said Adam.

"What I mean," she went on, "is that paradise is an attitude. If you assume the right attitude, paradise is here."

"The right attitude meaning lying down on 'cool mosses deep,' " I broke in sarcastically.

"Why not? Why else is the moss there?"

With that she knelt on the grass, curled up, and went to sleep. I should say, coiled up.

Adam stood looking down at her. "She's a night person," he said.

"You're the one who knows," I said.

She really was too long limbed and thin, bony and angular. I should think a man would want more flesh.

"The sun will hurt her," he said. "I'll have to fetch palm leaves."

"She has a nerve, lying there practically on the hearth of our home—next she'll be in it. Just as you had a nerve summoning her. I don't know which was worse, your hiding her or your flaunting her. Obviously the thing to do is to get her up and send her back to the shades where she belongs. Alone and palely loitering."

"She needs to sleep."

"I daresay. She wouldn't if you didn't deprive her of it at night. You didn't worry when I lost sleep over you."

"The sun will burn her."

"That will only improve her appearance. I have never seen anything so pale—in hair and skin and eyes. It's sickly. It's sickening. Even the zebra has stripes. Why would men prefer blondes?"

"They marry brunettes."

But I wasn't to be charmed and he wasn't to be stopped, for he ran off and came back with his arms full of palm leaves, which he laid on her as if she were dead, which I wished she were. He even positioned them on her head and the one cheek that was exposed. I felt like kicking her awake. I felt like kicking him, as he knelt ever so tenderly in undisguised worship. This, surely, was the sin of idolatry. Worship of a false goddess, as at an altar. In the days of our first love he had garlanded me, but not in worship. Now he was performing a ceremony of green caresses that now had reached her shamelessly flaunted buttocks, with the blonde tuft in between. Kiss me there, she seemed to demand, and in a way he did. Doubtless she was only pretending to be fast asleep, while enjoying every minute of it, including my humiliation. It must, at the very least, have tickled.

Speaking of kissing and tickling, I now have to relate something embarrassing. Lilith, under her green plumage, slept—or pretended to sleep—as if she were going to lie there forever. Adam and I, naturally, were on bad terms. Bad terms indeed!—that was the day he cleaved the apple and indulged in other sophistries. His mind had been darkened. He said marriage and morality were two entirely different things. His taking up with Lilith was not a moral question at all.

He would have done well to go off and forage, but I could see he feared to leave me alone with that dormant figure lest I wreak my wrath on it.

With nightfall I had had more than my fill. I told him I preferred to have my bed and the cave to myself. "Crawl up beside her, as you've been doing."

For all I know, that was what he did. In which case the mosquitoes left them severely alone. It being rather cool and damp in the cave, I undid the leopard skin and used it as a blanket. (On nights that now seemed long past we had lain uncovered and warmed each other.) All the upset that I had had pushed away sleep. That hussy (did she drug herself?) could drop like that for a day and more, in complete unperturbed relaxation, and I, with a good conscience, tossed and turned. It wasn't fair. She had charged me with insomnia, and now I had it.

At long last, after the moon had journeyed far from the entrance, I drifted off, only to be aroused by a tickling sensation in between my legs. It was nothing I had ever felt before. My somnolent mind wasn't functioning; my body was confused. Should it respond with a giggle? Before it could, it passed on to intense serious pleasure, waves and waves of it moving upwards, engulfing me to my breasts, which began to heave. I say waves advisedly, because the source was wet, not the dry touch of hand or penis—unless I myself was producing the wetness down there. I was being made love to as never before: that is, without the weight of a body on me, only hands on my thighs and a mouth—yes, it could only be a mouth—at my vital center. It was the most effective lovemaking since Eden. Adam was humbly—and overpoweringly—asking my forgiveness. The actions of his mouth, and his darting tongue deep within me, spoke louder than words, and would not be denied.

"Oh my dearest," I moaned, "you have come back to me." I was transported, confused, and out of myself. Feelings so new were too much for me. My heated and alarmed senses were in a tumult that robbed me of all liberty of thought. Tears of pleasure and gratitude gushed from my eyes and somewhat assuaged the fire that raged all over me. I reached down to pull him up. I liked him there—oh how I liked him there!—but I also wanted him on my breasts, his mouth on my mouth, and his proper part in me, as in the old beautiful days and nights.

As the worst of the venom left my lips, I thought, "If, despite his lies, he strips the wound from my soul with a kiss—I crawl his slave, soul, body and all!"

But the body that moved upwards and covered mine in the darkness was not his. "A paradise within thee, happier far," whispered the hated voice, caressing my locks.

I went cold and clammy. "Out, out, hyena, serpent, incubus," I ordered, wrenching her hand away.

"You mean succuba, don't you?" she mocked. "Silly confused creature, does it matter who sucks as long as the sucking is good?"

I pushed her away, and she slunk out, back to my husband, no doubt.

That tiny amount of sleep was all I was going to get. Thoughts stung me like hornets. There was, in the first place—or the last—her perversion of the word "good." That sucking of me, a peculiar sensation unknown in Eden, and never resorted to by my husband, was "good"? (Immediately after the so-called Fall he had asked, I remembered, for the equivalent from me.) It felt good.

Did the body ever lie? Was pleasure always a good? Such was Lilith's gospel. Was it the devil's? The body did not lie about pain. But if it was telling the truth about pleasure, I had to admit (to myself) that mine had been of the intensest as long as I thought my husband was the donor.

But that brought in the mind, which made it complicated. My body didn't seem to care who was doing the kissing. It just liked it. All of me liked it as long as I thought a repentant husband was making love to me. But *love*, like *good*, was a tricky word. Could there be love without physical pleasure, as there had been pleasure without love? He could love me and yet fail my body. That had happened a number of times before she came on the scene.

Ah, but I didn't really know how far back she dated. I couldn't prove that he loved me. He himself couldn't. Maybe his physical failure came because of diminished love. Yet that theory was to be weakened by his on the whole affectionate—but impotent—old age.

Beyond denial, she, whom I despised, could enchant my body. Perhaps her very technique had been a perversion, applying the wrong parts to the wrong places. We had been told to be fruitful and multiply. This practice thwarted that injunction. So it would be wrong, even from my husband.

In any case she had polluted that particular sexual approach forever. Probably that was her intention. I now had to rule it out for the rest of our lives. It might have been a consolation—a mutual consolation—in our old age. In truth, I missed it. There were thousands of days and nights when I longed for it. Another apple poisoned. It is a dreadful thing that I should remember it so vividly, against my will. Relive it and miss it.

By morning I was sick. I staggered out and vomited on the grass. The chest that had heaved in pleasure heaved in spasmodic agony. I felt as if I were being torn inside out. Three times, four times, when would it stop? I was forced, as if a hand pushed my head, to look down at and smell what I had done, and retch again. That is the inside of you, that is your supper, do you like it? Have some more. Ready for breakfast so you can do it again? This isn't abstract thought. This is the real inner yellow (that hateful color) nasty you. Lovable you. Embraceable you. Smell yourself. Take a good look. It's worse than that red stuff you exude every once in a while that makes Adam turn from you and gives you cramps. But that's not all that makes him turn from you. How can such a disgusting person ever expect to hold him? Your main opponent is you. Wretched retching you.

I hadn't noticed in my frantic rush whether they were lying there or not. When at last I was able to look, they were gone. Had I driven them away with my hideous cawing, or had they left earlier for the—to them comfortable—woods? I hoped the latter. Let it have been to them a distant noise at most, one more animal sound.

Could I live alone and like it? Enough food I expected I could find. There, lately, Adam had been negligent and selfish anyway. The cave and bed I had made—and proclaimed—mine. Could I lie alone and like it? Better than waiting for him. Sex was no further than my fingers' ends. They were expert beyond any man, potent or impotent. They knew exactly what to do and how long. As for conversation, is quarreling conversation?

There remained only the matter of being fruitful and multiplying. A pity that women needed a male for that. Did I want a child? What was a baby like? Why should I give birth "in sorrow"? I would evade the sentence, even as Adam (the great evader!) had pretty well succeeded in evading the sweat-of-thy-face curse. His face sweated more in copulation, I do believe. What could a child mean to me—trouble and care, judging by the animals. Why should the race be continued, especially with a playboy husband? Let him see what Lilith could produce, if anything. Rotten fruit.

So I nearly sent Adam away forever. It was pity, that base emotion, that led me to take him back. He told a pathetic, disturbing tale. Men are adept at that. He said he meant to creep into another cave for shelter, at least temporarily, since I had forbidden him mine. He made his way to the mouth of one and looked into it. His look was met by a yellowish glitter, two unblinking eyes, small, sharp, cold, shining out of the darkness but gliding with a smooth, steady motion towards the light and himself.

Suddenly it threw off the curse on snakes—"upon thy belly shalt thou go"—and erected itself for one-third of its man's length. It started balancing to and fro like a streaked brown and white flower in the breeze. It fanned out its head and neck, with the curiously beautiful markings, and darted a tongue the color of dried blood. It looked ready to bite, and as if that bite would be deadly above that of any beast of the field.

Adam stood transfixed, struck dumb, staring back helplessly with, I infer, dilating pupils and sudden numbness of fear that cannot move, as in the terror of dreams. The two sparks of light pushed forward until they grew to circles of yellow flame. He waited as in a trance, waited as one who longs to have the blow fall and be done with it. He waited for the prophesied death, the end of man.

But as he stared straight into the flaming eyes it seemed to him that they were losing their light and terror, that they were growing tame and dull. The charm was dissolving, the numbness was passing away. Adam could move once more. His ears picked up a song, faint and sweet, that was causing the cobra to sway in place, dancing its head and body about, keeping time to the music. Lilith had glided up alongside my husband, and sang away, and with her whitish eyes stared down, the danger.

"Serpent to serpent," I commented, repeating an insult that had been flung at me. " 'I will put enmity between thee and the woman,' " I quoted.

"She saved my life," he replied. "But our life together, that also must be saved."

"I don't exactly know why."

But I wasn't feeling very well, so he could press his advantage.

"I won't have any more lies," I told him. "I won't ask you to promise not to see her, because you'll break your promise and lie about it. On pretext of hunting you'll go off to be with her. I don't want to know and I don't want to see her. But you'll spend the nights with me, every night. Soon you will tire of her. That's certain and my only real protection."

At night I set out to be total woman to him, even licking him in not all, but some, surprising places. If she could seduce, why couldn't I. I had a better, more rounded, softer figure. Who wants bones in bed? Who wants crab apples for breasts? I was the first woman in the world, in every sense. I would prove it. I did prove it. I climbed all over him. I manipulated him to potency—it wasn't easy—and forced him to loud ecstasy. We slept skin to skin, and I don't mean leopard or cheetah.

All this contact was the reason, I thought, for the tenderness and enlargement of my breasts. Use an organ and it gets larger: Adam illustrated that beautifully. Use it a lot and it gets sore, too. My nipples hurt. They became impossible to touch. They and the skin around them grew darker. I had strange tinglings and throbbings long after my man had departed for, I sincerely hoped, foraging only. My breasts felt full, like udders. Had we overindulged?

The sickness after getting up was not always possible to conceal from him, hard as I tried. The best thing was to stay in bed and have him bring me something. When the call of nature sent me to the bushes, I felt dizzy. Even worse than vomiting were the empty spasmodic attempts: heaving to no avail. "What could have disagreed with you?" asked Adam. I imagined this food or that as the cause. I had a particular aversion to meat. I averted my gaze, self-protectively, when Adam smacked his lips over a bone. I wanted to hold my nose against the odor of roasting. I became a vegetarian. "You'll get thin," he said. "That is the shape you like," I said. "Or used to like."

But, after uncounted days, I got bigger. An ooze from my breasts replaced the occasional unpleasant flow below, as if the latter had been stanched. The veins in my legs burst under a new weight. Sexual intercourse became difficult. Standing, I couldn't make out my knees. I lay down on the grass and lifted them to make sure they were still there, with their dimples.

I had never witnessed a mammalian birth. The domestic arrangements of birds I admired, especially the dove. The male and female cooperated from beginning to end. A clever nest was constructed from sticks. Only one egg was laid, that white, not speckled. The redbreast that laid five eggs was overdoing it, I felt. When it came to sitting on the egg, one parent did it in the daytime, the other at night. At the hatching some sort of milk was found for the naked and blind young. The newborn was so helpless, so dependent, so nearly dead. I had seen a white-handed gibbon before and after pregnancy. I wished I had caught her in the process of birth. With her arms and legs she made her own nest around a small black-faced creature just like her, the same white circlet around the black, the same brown coat. They were a clean, gentle, and intelligent family of three, swinging with their long arms from tree to tree, their feet holding food. It was the next best thing to flying, my lost dream.

I recall no jolt of recognition. I cannot identify the moment when I realized what was wrong with me—or right with me, depending on the point of view. Maybe there never was a moment, but a slow uninsistent consciousness. I also do not know whether Adam was ahead of me in the realization. He may have been ashamed as the cause of it all, at the worst of times, his time of infidelity. Was she pregnant too? If normal, she was. Normal would certainly not be the first word I would apply to her, however.

I almost wanted to see her, for a glimpse of her belly. I had the impulse to question Adam. But that would be against my stern know-nothing resolution. I needed to insulate myself from outside worry. The worry inside sufficed.

We had consumed a boar before I gave up meat, the meanest animal I ever laid eyes on. I underwent another boar nightmare. This time the boar was inside me but tearing its way out, between my legs. Had I eaten it alive, or given birth to it? All the bleeding down below I had not done for months now poured forth in the dream, as the boar slashed its way out with its teeth and its tusks. I woke up in a pool of urine.

Adam snored beside me, unbothered. I would have to change the branches and the straw. Our marriage bed began with flowers of many hues, but they wilted too fast to be practical. Still, I had liked the fragrance while it lasted. Now I had to lie in and inhale my urine because I didn't want to disturb my husband, my lord and master. He was comfortable, unconcerned, apart from the whole trouble. He ran away when he felt like it and saw her if he pleased, while I moved about like a hippopotamus. Yet he was the cause, the unplanned cause.

That festered. I should have had a chance to make a decision, not be the victim of an accident, or a plot.

This had overtaken me without my consent or knowledge. It might as well have happened while I was asleep. It was a trap, a biological trap. Knowledge of good and evil: I had only surprise and fear. How—and when—would I deliver myself of this growing thing, this thing that split my sides and my veins, this thing that began to kick me—how was I to free myself without either my death or its, or both? I literally didn't see a way out. It was too big to ever get out. I would die with it inside. I should have killed it, somehow, while it was still small.

I felt like an animal, and a sick one at that. Hairiness proved kinship with the animals. Since our exile from Eden, Adam's human face divine was increasingly covered with a beard. I didn't like it. It tickled meaninglessly. I wanted him to pluck it out but I knew from experiment on myself that that hurt. The hair of my head was now dank and lifeless, its sheen gone. I felt thoroughly unattractive. We could no longer make love. Was *she* still her trim blonde self? On my abdomen was a new ridge of hair. It was there that I made the plucking experiment but couldn't go through with it. But much greater pain awaited me, according to the prophecy, the curse.

It was hard for me to believe that God was on my side, blessing me with increase. The so-called Fall was supposed to be the consequence of free will, not deceit. I felt that I had again been tricked. It was for me to say if I wanted a baby, not have it thrust upon me at risk to life and mental and emotional equilibrium. "We freely choose," repeated my pious husband, who still claimed to receive instruction from heaven. He freely chose to be a philanderer, an adulterer, and an impregnator, I suspect, of more than one woman. I'd have liked to know what I was freely choosing. When we finally acknowledged my situation to each other, he threw his arms to the skies in a ridiculous manner and shouted gleefully, "You have gotten a man from the Lord!"

"I thought it was from you," I said.

"There are primary causes and secondary causes."

"How do you know it will be a man? Because it's big and restless and dangerous?"

"I know. I am given to know."

"What's wrong with a girl?"

"A boy is better. You will see."

I saw. . . . Adam named him Cain, which meant, Adam said, metalworker, because he was going to be the originator of science and invention, of all progress, beginning with agriculture.

I cannot bear witness to the birth. I can only darkly conjecture. Water broke in me. I had terrible pain, unbearable, the worst in my life, then trouble breathing. Lying on the grass, Adam beside me, I passed out. When I came to, a male baby was at my side, the umbilical cord severed and knotted. He didn't look like much, but then they seldom do.

When I took it to my breast, it bit me. Examination revealed two lower central incisors. For all I knew, that was normal, but Abel and Seth proved it wasn't.

"Aren't you glad it isn't a girl?" gloated Adam.

THREE

"Lilith is gone. I swear to you."

Once you have been lied to, can you ever believe again? I almost feel sorry for liars. What can they do to be convincing when, as will happen sooner or later, they have a truth they wish to convey? One can't get through a lifetime without having occasion to say something that is true and wanting to be believed. It may be something quite trivial to the other person, such as, "I have a pain in my side." But it matters to you and it matters whether you get help or not. I thought of telling Adam a story (a story is not a lie) about a boy crying for help from a vicious animal, say a wolf, but every time it was a lie—there was no wolf—until the last time, when it was true, and nobody came to his rescue because he had fooled them too often.

Adam had fooled me too often. I couldn't trust his words. It was very sad that I couldn't. He would have to tell a lot of verifiable truths—in important areas—before I could begin to believe him again, and even then my believing might be selective. Using stronger language, such as "I swear" (with hand on heart and eye to heaven—a silly posture, but then I have no gift for piety) might only be an effort to improve the lying style after milder presentations had met with skepticism.

I couldn't trust his words, but probably I could trust his actions. I mean his sexual action. After Eden, Adam's potency was, as I have indicated, very finite. With two women he ran short fast. I was able to tell, when we commenced making love again after the birth, I was able to tell from his ardor that he was no longer a bigamist, that I was the sole recipient of his attentions. Maybe they had quarreled. Maybe she had returned to her side of the mountain, or her demonic place of origin. A pleasure-seeker like that is easily bored. Maybe she only wanted a child from him—and got it. She'd never get one from that fit mate—her brother?—of horrible memory who sodomized me.

So—just Adam and me, and baby makes three, in my blue heaven. We could be as happy as gibbons.

But the gibbon reproduced the spitting—and I mean spitting—image of the gibbon. This drooling creature at my side resembled neither me nor Adam. Like an animal, it was covered all over with fuzzy hair. A thick blond crop occupied the scalp and forehead. Its face was waxen, puffy, and lumpy. Its head was misshapen, elongated at the back, and lopsided. The skull had one soft spot and one ugly dark lump, as if it had been banged. It bobbled on a rubbery neck, but it cried in complaint when I held it. Its eyes, so loose that they crossed, didn't see us. Its nipping at my nipples was an unendurable waste. Neither my love nor my milk was flowing.

If it had required either the first days, it would have perished. But it had a persistent drive to live, yelling and waving its arms and screwing up its little monkey face. Exhausted, it slept. After three days I had milk for it. Each time it bit I slipped my fingers between its gums and admonished, "No." I was sorry the first word it heard was negative, but it was a battle of wills. It would either learn or starve. It was greedy for as much of my breast as it could engorge. It learned to suck without biting, but once satisfied, it thanked me with a nip. It was as if I had a snake in my bosom. My nipples went from sore to cracked. But it hurt, also, not to be milked. We needed each other, whether we liked each other or not. Once, in desperation, I asked Adam to suck me, but he didn't know how, lacked a certain fold the baby had in its lip.

Adam was rather standoffish, literally—inclined to look down, bemused. He seemed uncomfortable, embarrassed, with what he had caused. The nearest to a gesture of love on his part was to stick his little finger in the baby's hand, which did not close on it. "You give him too much attention," he complained. My husband didn't like being waked up in the middle of the night. He didn't like to have him between us in bed. I didn't either, for a different reason: I was afraid one of us in our sleep would roll over him and crush him. I made a separate bed of branches for him. The cave was small. I wanted to look for a bigger one but the cobra story scared me.

Cain was so helpless for so long. Would he had remained so! I didn't expect much for a long while from his limbs, but I wondered about his speech. Baby animals didn't sound greatly different from their parents. On this analogy Cain should have been uttering words. It would have helped immensely if I had known his thoughts, his needs. His yowls could mean anything, hunger, pain, anger.

As the cycles of the moon repeated, Cain's eyes lost their vacancy, he looked at us, he supported his own head, he sat up, he accepted a berry. There came the time when he no longer needed my breast nor my breast him. I trickled coconut milk to him. We had played with these hairy balls, Adam and I, without dreaming there was anything good inside until one split open. Cain added upper teeth to his lower.

On coming in from tending the fire I discovered he had pulled the parental bed apart. Long past the early mewing, he crowed and squealed. I watched with curiosity when a toad hopped within his range. Would he be afraid? He wasn't afraid of ants. Sitting up, he scooped the toad with both hands and squeezed, squeezed with admirable muscle. Then he parted his hands and let the squashed animal fall. "Dead," he said. That was the first word he ever uttered. (Abel's first word was "Ma," Seth's "Dada.") Adam, who had been in the woods, chose to be skeptical. "Probably he said 'Dad.' " I know what I heard.

From an early age Cain was fascinated by the fire. He inveigled ants and spiders and beetles to mount a stick, which he then pushed into the fire. When he could walk without staggering, Adam took him hunting. Cain was the first to employ a sharp stick for pinning down trapped animals. He was in no hurry to kill them, as Adam always was. A later development was to throw the stick. With the thing came, as always, the right word: spear. Once he pushed a weeping willow on top of an already dead hare, squashing it to uselessness. (The guts were never our favorite part.) The word for this was overkill.

"I want another child," I informed my husband. "I want this one to be on purpose."

"It seems to be God's will, whether we get one or not," he said. "We have never not tried."

You forget the time you tried with Lilith rather than with me, I thought, but prudently held my tongue.

My growing belly finally gave notice. I underwent no morning sickness, thanks be to God. "This is a good omen. Since it doesn't make me sick it will probably be a girl," I exulted. "In any case I do the naming this time—Abel, meaning breath, breath of life."

This time I was able to continue eating meat. Roast

lamb was my favorite, gazelle meat being hard to come by. The sheep had increased and multiplied and their habit of flocking made them easy to find on the hills. Cain enjoyed pricking them with his spear until they bleated and bled. Once he stuck it into the eye of a lamb. Another time, when a fledgling redbreast glided to earth, he placed his sturdy foot on it and crushed it. I tried, unsuccessfully, to teach him there was no point in killing what we didn't want to eat or torturing what we weren't ready to kill for food.

Also, like his father, he could be sneaky and untruthful. I had the uneasy feeling that he stared at us in the darkness as we made love. I would break off and crawl towards his little bed and at once he would pretend to snore. But he never snored at any other time. For a small child he slept much less than I thought he should. In the daytime he stared rather than spoke, like a wary animal, with his pale milky eyes (the original blue had faded). The white showed below the iris. It did not with Adam. It did not with me. His complexion was not that of either of us. But a barefaced—or should I say a white-faced—lie came easy to him. One dawn in the cave I played a trick similar to his. I watched under glimmering eyelids while he, after staring at us, got up and stole from a crevice a bunch of grapes, an unabundant delicacy, that I had kept refrigerated for all of us for breakfast. Greedily he engorged without restraint, popping them in fast until only the stems remained, his eyes on me the whole while. It was a squirrel's wary attitude and he had squirrel's teeth.

Don't say anything. Don't let on you saw him. It is a terrible thing to be watched. You don't like him watching you. That is what is frightening about the Almighty, the Omniscient, the Big Eye in the Sky. It's not a sin to be hungry. What will he do with the stems?

He put the stems back where the grapes had been. So—one deception begets another—I had, when we all got up, to put my hand in and draw out the stems with great surprise. "What happened to our grapes? Cain, have you any idea who ate the grapes?" "No, mommy." A heave of the little shoulders. "Must have been an animal, mommy."

You little rodent, you.

I think I handled it well. But my coming child would be honest. It was a planned child. Willed, not wild. You couldn't expect much from an accident. Instead of an aggressive troublesome boy I'd have a sweet girl with my long brown hair and violet eyes. For all I knew—for all I know—a girl is born with hair down to her hips.

With Abel I had just a few quick labors. He slid out with the waters, slippery, easy. The contractions came early in the morning while the two males were asleep, yes, even Cain, I believe. But he was as watchful as the light allowed when I asked Adam to feel my abdomen as it went alternately hard and soft. Adam, with one hand on me, looked at the child. "He mustn't see this," he said.

"I may need your help," I said, "especially if I faint again."

His answer was, "No, you'll be all right, you'll be fine. I have to get the boy out of here. Call if you need anything." And he grabbed Cain's arm and hurried with him out of the cave.

I separated the newborn with my teeth, joined him with my breast.

Yes, this baby was mine, clearly mine, from beginning to end. He had my nose. After his black hair came out he grew in brown, as if deciding to take after me instead of his father. There was nothing waxen or misshapen about this beautiful boy, my planned pride and joy, the apple of my eye. He responded to my love from the very start. I can't remember that Cain ever gurgled or cooed or smiled.

"We should prepare Cain for the blessed happening," I had said. "He has already asked what's wrong with my stomach."

"And what did you say?"

"I said I'm not sick, just getting bigger."

"It is embarrassing. At four he's not ready for a full explanation. No pun intended. We could say babies are found in caves."

"And have him go searching for one and be bitten by a snake?"

78

"We could say the vulture brings it."

"That's not funny. Why shouldn't I get the credit that I'm due?"

"All right. Leave me out."

"He peeps so much that he likely already has some idea of your part."

Your private part, which isn't very private. The only time I bared myself to Cain was when we all bathed and played in the stream. He did a lot of staring then, but never asked questions. He took to snatching at his father, snatching at his father's penis. "Big, big, big," he repeated. Adam had to stop him because it hurt. The boy had strong hands and arms as well as untiring legs that enabled him to go wherever his father led him. You could foresee a great explorer, a wanderer over the earth, which was why I didn't want him poking into any caves.

Late in the morning when the two males came in for the first look I still felt the sweat on me but the baby was contentedly asleep and I was drowsy myself. I didn't want words or noise. Peace, peace! Dost thou not see my baby at my breast, that sucks the nurse asleep?

"It's dead," said Cain in a voice that echoed through the cave.

"Of course not," answered his father. "Your brother Abel sleeps."

Our habitation was now too small, if it hadn't been before. After eating, Adam left to look for a bigger cave. We had discussed this imminent problem before, but evidently for him in nonreligious matters seeing was believing—not with God but with God's gifts. He would use a firebrand against the possibility of snakes. Because of that danger and because of the expected roughness of the exploration, Cain was left behind to play at the entrance of our home. I drowsed off, my baby at my side.

It is given to mothers to sleep lightly. The smallest sound arouses them, and a tiny brief cry aroused me, the smallest squeak of the smallest animal. My arm felt the baby was gone before my eyes saw. They darted to Cain sitting with Abel facing his chest, arms wound around the baby and tightening. The neck looked broken.

"What are you doing?" I shouted, startling him into relaxing his grip and even handing back the baby, now terribly silent, and red, and bleeding at the navel. I held him upside down and slapped his back and got him breathing again. I stanched the wound with herbs. Cain sat staring. "You nearly killed him," I finally was able to tell him. "No, no, no," he said. "Hug, hug, hug."

That was my first warning, and I heeded it. I took all possible precautions. A baby can so easily perish anyway, of itself. And little children can bring accidents on themselves. "God should have skipped childhood," observed Adam. "I'm sure he did," I answered, "as we did. But I wouldn't want an adult bursting me at the seams.

Abel was happily smaller than Cain." "I think elephants are pregnant longer" came the clumsy consolation. "Wreathing the lithe proboscis?" I asked.

Downstream we found a two-bedroom cavern. Cain was given his own room. This home was damper than the previous one, and of course the inner room, which we took for ourselves and the baby, was darker. This had advantage and disadvantage, the advantage being that no matter how hard Cain tried to peer at us with his pale eyes he saw less, while we could keep better watch on him. As before, we counted on the fire to keep out snakes and other pests, but I kept a nervous eye on crevices that were big enough for green- or yellow-tongued vipers, at least until pebble-reinforced mud blocked that possibility. Adam had argued that we ourselves should be near the entrance to guard it, but my wish for privacy—and a measure of relief from one particular pest—prevailed. "The restless boy can go in and out without stumbling past us." I had to concentrate on my baby and his needs.

Abel was sickly and slow to gain weight. A few days after the double trauma of birth and Cain's hug, he, who had been so good, commenced crying and didn't stop. It was evening. We were all home. I turned him over, patted him, gave him a drink of water, but nothing worked. His abdomen was distended, as if pregnant. He stiffened his legs. He emitted from below a foul odor. "He stinks," said his brother.

"I want to sleep. Shut him up." I worried that my milk was bad.

This worry gnawed at me because the crying commenced right after a breast feeding. I—who had meant to nourish—gave pain and death? He was crying his life out. His tiny legs were already laid out like a corpse. He would die of exhaustion if not of poison. He wailed out his life-force. Adam fell to his knees and prayed. I almost longed for Lilith, any woman to proffer advice. Finally my breast was ready again and I stopped him with that.

But the next night was the same, and the next, and the next, through three moons. Only I now knew that it would always end, in the same way, with my bad milk turning to good milk: bad once a day, at all other times good. Or was there something about the late-afternoon visits of his brother that upset him, that impassive stare? Should Cain be forbidden our bedroom? He had no reason to be there. If only Abel could have absorbed some of his sturdy health! Cain was so independent, so above—or below—love. He possessed an almost hideous strength.

"I've seen jealousy in you," remarked my husband, "and he has it too."

"There's no comparison. I wasn't jealous. I was right."

He smiled, in his superior way. His smile wasn't what it used to be in his beardless days. "Cain—and I must say I—can't help but feel it when all your loving care goes in one direction."

"I give it where it's needed."

"Maybe he cries in order to get it."

"That's a shocking statement. He cries because he's in pain."

"You said there shouldn't be two wives. Maybe there shouldn't be two children."

"We were told differently from above, according to you. And by the way, *you* displayed jealousy of Cain when he was a baby. So that means no children. I wanted this one, and I cherish him, in sickness and in health."

"Till death do us part."

"You're as funny as a dead hyena."

I watched my baby anxiously. He did grow. Adam agreed that he did. When at last he got over whatever caused his agonizing crying, I was free to study him for signs of normal development in sucking, looking, listening, vocalizing, grasping, moving. At three moons he could follow moving objects with his eyes. His favorite objects were his own hands. "That's you," I informed him as the little fists passed like slow birds before his line of vision. I think he was under the impression they belonged to someone else. The fingers of one hand discovered the fingers of the other and were delighted. Gurgles of pleasure. He smiled when I came within view, as Cain never did. He joyfully knew me. He reacted to my voice. He liked to sit up and look around, master of all he surveyed. He was sweet as an orange, he was trusting. He had no reason to believe anything could hurt him.

Came the day he lowered his dimpled chin to let out "Ma" as I was dandling him. "He would have said Da if it had happened to be I who was holding him," claimed his father, who saw and heard and couldn't deny. But Adam had to wait quite a while for *his* signal. Abel was definitely mother's boy.

I needed to be eternally vigilant against his rough, tough brother. I feared that two-legged animal more than anything on fours. Cain appeared to have no understanding of how frail a baby is. Or did he know very well? Not only would he have hugged him to death, he almost frightened him to death.

This happened when Abel was approximately eight moons old. We were sitting around the fire, my baby and I, in the late afternoon, basking in the no longer too hot sun, after a nap. Our bedroom was safe enough, with me such a light sleeper and Abel on the far side of the inner room. Outside was safe as long as Cain was roaming the woods and fields with his father. Adam had noted with fatherly pride, "Our little man is a born hunter. He really enjoys going after those animals, even the ones we can't eat, like the monkeys. I suppose he wants to improve his skill. His spear has blood on it all the time." I knew all I wanted to know about that.

I was wondering what food they would bring back this time, when, from nowhere, Cain advanced on the baby holding a gray wolf's head to his face. His fingers were by the black snout, lifting up the lips to bare the fangs. Blood dripped on his chest. He didn't give out a growl. He just silently came before the baby, as I leapt up to stop him.

Abel's face went as dead as the wolf's. Then came the slow pucker, then the full-lunged howling that continued long after I had literally kicked Cain off the scene and into the woods. "I don't want to see you until it's too dark to see you."

The head, which had been dropped, I tried to scoop away with a stick. I wasn't about to touch it. The eyes came up staring in every position. I threw a leafy branch over it and returned to my baby whom nothing would comfort. It was like the old illness, the old pain, back again—and at the same darkening time. But at least his heart hadn't stopped as it might have. Crying was life—that was the way to look at it. He was so much stronger than half a year ago. That much had been proven.

Rock-a-bye, baby, thy cradle is green. No, your mother's brown arms. Hush, hush. Where is Adam? Bye, baby bunting, Daddy's gone a-hunting, to get a little rabbit skin to wrap the baby bunting in.

He was still gasping when Adam came up. The little heart pounded against mine.

"What's wrong with him?"

"There's nothing wrong with him. There's a lot wrong with Cain. He nearly killed him—again."

I related what had happened.

"He has to play," Adam apologized. "When we found the dead wolf—actually it was still alive, had been mauled, and Cain finished him off—the boy asked me to help him get the head off. I sent him on ahead with his plaything. For you we have venison. Where is he?"

As if he understood, Abel wailed louder. We had to shout to be heard, which does nothing for calm conversation. "I really can't talk now," I yelled.

Adam pulled at my arm. "Set him down. Night has come." (That was an exaggeration.) "Is Cain in the cave?"

"No—he went—I don't know where."

"You didn't watch. You didn't notice. You didn't stop him. You don't in fact care."

"The animals have more reason to fear him than he them."

"What did you say?"

I repeated it, at the top of my voice. Abel, sensing the quarrel, gave us the top of his.

"Callous!" his father shouted. "And untrue. The boy is five, not that. Alone and lost in the woods, and probably afraid to come back anyway."

This was a neat way, oh very neat way, to put me in the wrong, to shift the blame from where it belonged.

Adam darted off in the direction of the forest as if Lilith, his Kalee, had summoned him. I was sure Cain would be found skulking behind some nearby tree. I carried my baby into our bedroom. He had to be protected from another sight of his brother, mask or no mask. I worked on soothing him, murmuring to him, singing a little. He took my nipple. At last he fell asleep, his breath a series of sighs through the nose that was my nose.

The hunter and the hunted returned soon enough, just as I had expected. They weren't even quiet. "Stay out there. Don't come in," I said to the boy and felt like saying to the man. Adam laid himself down beside me and was immediately amorous, even though we hadn't had dinner. I put aside the hand that not long before had touched me in violence. "It's not the right time."

"It's never the right time," Adam replied. "Cain is watching. You're too pregnant. You're menstruating. You hurt. You're tired. Baby is asleep. Baby has to have his milk. There's always some excuse, isn't there?" He started to get up, but now I grasped him, catching his leg.

"We'll talk it over tonight," I promised.

I was so upset that I feared my milk would go sour. I didn't arise to eat. I had no appetite. I lay by my frightened son, whose legs twitched as if bad dreams were pursuing him. Ought I to wake him? Would it be better to waken him, even if he then cried? I knew what the terror must have been, that wolf-face, the fangs, the blood (whose?), the fixed eyes no better dead than living. It would have petrified me on a body full-grown and at first sight unrecognized. I recalled how I felt when Adam came upon me suddenly disguised as a leopard. Like father, like son. It wasn't play, what Cain did. He meant to terrify. He knew he would. The deadly hug could have been overzealous—though I doubted it. The wolf-mask was telling the beastly truth. A truth that had to be faced (so to speak) and dealt with.

We discussed it in the middle of the night, as the rain poured down hard. On such occasions we moved a bit of fire just under the roof of the entrance. If necessary, Cain's bedroom could turn into a kitchen. But smoke could be a problem, depending on the wind. Some solution needed to be worked out for that. I cooked outside as much as possible, which was most of the time. If the inside fire died out, we always had a supply of dry sticks for rekindling. The animals kept out anyway. There was only little wolf-mask within. I hoped he hadn't retrieved it.

"With the children we've lost all our privacy," complained Adam. "You make me whisper even though the rain is loud."

"I'm not afraid of waking the baby. All the soothing finally took. He won't stir now till he's hungry. It's the eavesdropper we have to be careful about."

"Eve dropped him, all right."

"I've heard that pun before."

"It's a profound one. You dropped him in birth, but now you drop him from your love."

"It is hard to believe he is my own flesh and blood—he's so strange."

Adam had his arms around me, but now he let go and leaned on one arm, and his words came sharp and loud like a slap. "Don't say that!"

"I have to say what I feel and what I don't feel."

"The boy's jealousy is fully justified. He sees how Abel receives all your love. His mischief-making could be a desperate way of calling attention to himself. He feels your coldness towards him. When have you taken him into your arms?"

"He doesn't come. He's a hunter."

"He's trying to be a man. And a clever man. You should see the flint fist hatchet he made yesterday. He let me use it on the wolf."

"So that was what you had in your hand when you returned? Always weapons. What weapon do you need against a sheep? I think that's the only meat I'm going to want from now on."

"The boy is growing into a man, as he should. He wants to be big and strong like his father. He wants my penis. He wants your love."

There was something more than a little disturbing about these words, which left me silent.

Finally I said, "Tomorrow I will tell Cain a story, an animal story, a story with a lesson. He speaks so little. Maybe I don't speak enough to him. All action—not enough words, no understanding."

Whereupon my husband and I, naked under the catskin covers, turned to each other in our leafy bed and performed to mutual satisfaction an action that Cain couldn't, an action that brought at least temporary understanding and peace, without—and beyond—words. After, lullabied by the wind and the rain, we slept on our backs like the baby in his crib, till morning came and he opened his eyes and cried for milk.

After waiting for the nursing to be over, Adam said, "Let's hear the story. It will be the first man-made story ever."

"You've never told one? In any case, woman-made."

I was bearing the baby into Cain's room when Adam put his hand up. "Leave him here, can't you? This should be all Cain's, at least once."

The boy was prone, uncovered, his hard little buttocks staring up at us. He turned his head for a wary wide-eyed glance (when did I ever catch him asleep?) and reached for the sheepskin cover on the floor before flinging himself on his back. I got the impression he had been playing with his penis, which perhaps was stiff. Did he work at making it big like Daddy's? Did he ever glimpse Daddy's at its biggest? I hoped not. I addressed my first words to him since I had kicked him away.

"Cain dear, let me tell you about a wolf and a lamb that talked to each other. Animals do talk to each other, you know, though in a different language from ours. The lamb stood quenching its thirst in a river. A hungry wolf saw him and wanted an excuse for eating him. Standing higher up the river, he spoke furiously to the lamb, 'Why are you muddying the water so that I cannot drink?' The lamb replied, 'I am only drinking with the tip of my tongue. Besides, since I am standing lower down the river from you, I cannot possibly be disturbing the water higher up.' When this excuse failed, the wolf tried another. 'Don't you remember how you insulted me a year ago?' The lamb answered, 'I wasn't even born then.' Then the wolf said, 'If it wasn't you it was your brother, which is the same thing.' 'I don't have a brother,' answered the poor lamb. 'You talk too much,' said the wolf, and pounced on the lamb and devoured him."

"I wish *I* didn't have a brother," said Cain.

Adam looked at me. "Whatever you were up to, it didn't work."

I wanted to reply but couldn't in Cain's presence. When you have a child, there should be a place to send it to in the daytime. Having children, I cannot repeat too often, is the end of privacy. I even stayed longer in the bushes than I had to, to savor the privacy. The time was coming when Abel would be too big and too observant and too comprehending for our bedroom, even if he happily lacked his brother's furtive curiosity. Were there three-bedroom caves?

Tell a good story, and someone criticizes it. Adam

criticized mine in bed that night. "Your fable—I suppose that's what it was—isn't true to life. Talking animals! What are you teaching him?"

"Animals do communicate. They understand each other very well, sometimes better than we with all our fancy vocabulary do."

"Misled by you, the boy will start talking to the animals now."

"Let him look up and speak to the birds. I do sometimes. You should have heard me this afternoon, when a certain chattering became too much. 'My sisters the swallows,' I said, 'it is now time for me to speak, for you have said enough. Give me a chance.' "

"I'd have worried about you if I had heard you."

"No, talking to the animals will be better for Cain than not talking at all. He's much too silent, brooding, holding back. And it's an improvement on killing all the time."

"Your fable has killing in it."

"So it's true to life after all."

"But who's the wolf, who's the sheep? He'll fear it's about him and his baby brother. He had the wolf's head. He even has the skinned sheep. You're putting a terrible fear into him."

"Better act it out in imagination than do it for real. My story was a lesson, a lesson that cruelty won't listen to reason, that the cruel impulse in him is unreasonable but we all have to see it and restrain it."

"Don't be so sure that he's the wolf. You may figure as the wolf to him, withdrawing your love, punishing, unpredictable."

"I am perfectly predictable. If he's bad he will feel my hand or my foot."

"And your love—when does he feel that?"

"He has, in the first place, to be lovable."

Adam himself was taught a lesson the next morning. We woke up to a black stench, one that had become commonplace since Eden but that had never got into the cave before, the home that I kept clean and neat, scrubbing the floors with wet leaves and collecting sweet-smelling flowers and mints daily—I know a bank where the wild thyme blows—with which I lined the walls. This smell was not that of bowel movement, though that could be distinguished too: the baby lay serenely asleep in, as usual, his own evacuation. (Cain called him stinker.) Superimposed—and wafting from the other direction—was the unmistakable stench of animal decay.

We entered the front room and Cain was again on his stomach, with his eyes open, and he did not turn over and the stench came directly from him. My heart skipped a beat. Had some terrible affliction visited him? Adam ordered, "Get up," but the boy did not obey. He had his arms around the branches of his bed. His father pulled him up by the bare waist, the branches came apart, and the wolf's head was exposed, white seamed, its muzzle aswhirl with little crawling things and the eyes turned to maggots, and the stink alone enough to make me sway on my feet.

"Mine!" shouted the boy, standing between his father and the bed. He lowered his head like a goat about to butt. When Adam advanced, the child protested, "No, no, no," and swung into action with his fists, starting at the belly, then hitting further down. The cheetah skin was insufficient protection, for Adam gave a yell of pain and put his hands on his groin. Cain took a step back and glared. "Hate, hate, hate! I hate you." At this pause I sneaked behind them and snatched up the disgusting object and—not looking at it, trying not to feel my fingers sinking into its mush—cast it on the fire.

Cain was punished by being forbidden to leave his room. Adam and I conferred that morning outside, some distance away. I had my baby with me of course.

"What he needs is religion," said the father. "I will put the fear of God in him. I will teach him how in the beginning God created the heaven and the earth and every living thing, and caused the earth to bring forth grass, the herb yielding seed, and the fruit tree yielding fruit after its kind."

"I don't think you should mention fruit trees."

"We are all sinners and should confess as much."

So Adam summoned the boy and had us kneel on the grass and repeat after him as follows: "Almighty and most merciful Father, we have erred, and strayed from Thy ways like lost sheep. We have followed too much the devices and desires of our own hearts. We have offended against Thy holy laws. We have left undone those things which we ought to have done. And we have done those things which we ought not to have done. And there is no health in us. But Thou, O Lord, have mercy upon us, miserable sinners. Spare Thou those, O God, who confess their faults. Restore Thou those who are penitent."

He added, as if in reference to the forbidden tree, "All the things that God would have us do are hard for us to do—remember that—and hence, he oftener commands us than endeavors to persuade. And if we obey God, we must disobey ourselves; and it is in this disobeying ourselves wherein the hardness of obeying God consists."

So—to summarize, now, years and years—Adam turned into a preacher. He spoke of the beauty of holiness. He set aside every seventh day for morning worship. He would wear a garland of white flowers on these occasions—any species, water lily, kalanchoe, ixora, daisy, scaevola, provided it was white, white for purity. I refrained from pointing out how white—and impure—Lilith had been. The towhead boy grew in strength—and unruliness. He obeyed himself—that was whom he obeyed.

When he cut off the tail of Abel's pet squirrel, so that

it bled to death, Adam gave him hell. "The God that holds you over the pit of Hell, much as one holds a spider, or some loathsome insect, over the fire, abhors you, Cain, and is dreadfully provoked. His wrath towards you burns like fire; He looks upon you as worthy of nothing else but to be cast into the fire. He is of purer eyes than to bear to have you in His sight. You have offended Him infinitely more than ever a stubborn boy did his father. And yet 'tis nothing but His hand that holds you from falling into the fire every moment: 'tis to be ascribed to nothing else that you did not go to Hell the last night; that you were suffered to wake again in this world, after you closed your eyes to sleep: and there is no other reason to be given why you have not dropped into Hell since you arose in the morning. Now I lay me down to sleep, I pray the Lord my soul to keep. If I should die before I wake, I pray the Lord my soul to take. O sinner! Consider the fearful danger you are in."

"Shit, all shit!" muttered the ten-year-old boy, head lowered. I was the only one who heard it. I didn't know where he got his vocabulary from. Abel never let out a word like that.

Abel's mouth was sweet from milk, which his brother rejected at an early age. I nursed him until, at three, he got a bit heavy and I tired of the jeers of the others. Then I squeezed the elusive teats of sheep for him, proffering it still warm in a coconut cup. He didn't care for coconut milk.

That was the start of his fondness for the woolen flock. He wanted to be by them as they grazed. He touched their black noses, played with their floppy ears, and ran his fingers through their greasy coats. He cried over every slaying and refused the meat. "Mutton they are, Abel, and to mutton they must return," I consoled.

"Don't be blasphemous," said Adam.

I can't say I was ever religious compared to my black-haired white-chapleted husband with the solemn beard. He was deadly serious about his Sabbath observances, which didn't seem to improve anyone's conduct. Nor did Cain, already obsessed with death, need a sermon on the subject that dilated on corruption and putrefaction and vermiculation, envisioning the time when our mouths shall be filled with dust and the worms shall feed sweetly upon us. It was in response to that that I offered up my little joke about mutton.

We were unable to find a bigger cave, sorely needed. The two boys—had one of them been what a boy should be—would have slept together in the same room. But I wasn't trusting Abel to the tender mercies of a bully now grown too strong for me and in fact a match for his father. Cain was in the habit of challenging his father to a naked wrestle. These encounters got less and less playful. In the beginning it was "the manly art of self-defense" that Adam proposed to teach the pubic-haired teenager. Defense against whom, I couldn't imagine. It wasn't suitable for animals. I believe Adam was glorying in his strength in a childish way and even the toughness and resilience—ever increasing—of his son, just as he used to run him off his legs, or prowl with him to exhaustion. Testing what a fine strong body had developed from his seed. He didn't worry enough, despite his sermons, about the mind and character. Feel the biceps. Feel the flying tackle or the squirm to break a headlock. I found it rather indecent, the penises flying. And when Adam got him down it looked like sexual conquest. Why couldn't they cover their loins with something besides each other?

Adam was tall and narrow, his bones were very thin and fine. Cain was squat, stocky, heavy at the thighs. They seemed to drive their brown flesh deeper and deeper against each other, as if they would break into a oneness. Came the day, inevitably I suppose, when Cain got his father down. At nineteen he tripped him, they rolled over and over on the grass and stopped with Cain on top. Their eyes fastened on each other not in love. Adam was straining to lift his outspread arms staked to earth by thick wrists and massive hands. Cain rode Adam's tossing hips until all opposition ceased except an uplifted head and the irate command, "Get off." The victor wasn't going to abandon his pleasure that fast. He sat astride and cocked his head at me and his wide smirk declared as plainly as words, "So much for the first of men!"

That proved to be his declaration of independence, for that afternoon he moved into his own cave with his own fire. It was nearby—I wish it hadn't been. He became a tiller of the ground. With a stick he turned over the earth and planted barley seed, which he watered when the rain didn't. I never cared for the mush he made by grinding and mixing it with water. Adam declared that he was very clever and that this was progress. There would eventually be no need for foraging. I felt any activity closest to Eden was the best, finding whatever God or nature gave us.

Around this time, true to his name, Cain showed us a few shining beads of metal. He had banked his fire with pieces of copper ore lying about. Roasted, the metal had been precipitated from the stone. I remarked how nice the beads (at last something that didn't decay) would look strung somehow around my neck. Cain said they would make good tips for a spear. He was going to try for larger pieces, a whole spear, tip and shaft of copper. He foresaw a glittering future in weaponry.

Abel, fifteen, moved to the front room. Having him all those years in our bedroom did reduce our privacy, although he mostly slept like a baby when he was well and never had Cain's staring curiosity. Slender like his father, with my complexion, he often wasn't well. I nursed him through a number of fevers, laying cold compresses on his forehead as he tossed his curls from side to side or lifted himself up in spasm. In delirium he cried mysteriously, "Don't, don't!" He was also, like me, subject to occasional nightmares but refused to describe them. That was *his* privacy, I guess. Once he cut his foot on a rock and it swelled beyond recognition and yellow stuff kept leaking from it. "Looks as if it will have to be cut off," remarked Cain, but I bathed it and put healing herbs on it—narcissus root proved the most effective for the unbroken skin—and eventually the boy could limp around.

Abel was an experienced keeper of sheep. He showed an affinity for these creatures at such an early age that I called him my lambikin. Actually a newborn lamb is not easily cradled. Its four ungainly legs are big, about as big as they are ever going to get. I remember Abel carrying one to save it. It had slipped from its dam apparently lifeless. Abel took it from the field and laid it beside our fire. After a time the lamb, revived by the warmth, began to bleat, and Abel returned it to its mother. "You would make a loving father," I complimented him, running my fingers through his hyacinthine locks.

(Is Seth, my dying hope, a loving father? I advised him, if he had a son, to name it Enos, which means teacher.)

The day so many sheep died was the day Abel, my "breath of life," died, age sixteen. We all blamed ourselves for what happened, that is, all but one of us did. The murderer mocked, "Am I my brother's keeper?"

Abel blamed himself for what happened to his flock. He had had stomach cramps, as so often, debilitating attacks that caused his brother to poke him and jeer, "You must be pregnant." Kept awake most of the night, he overslept in the morning. When he got up to look to his sheep, the stupid ewes had strayed into the dewy young clover and eaten it. Is there anything as stupid as sheep? If one goes over a cliff—and I've seen that happen—they all go over the cliff. Follow the leader to blind doom.

Abel's cries of consternation brought Adam and me running. Many of the animals were lying on their sides. Others dropped as we watched. Swollen with wind and the rank mist they drew, they foamed at the mouth. Their breathing came quick and short, those that breathed at all. Their bodies were doubled in size.

Abel was feeling the flank of one. "It's air. They've taken in air. It has to be let out or they will all die." He looked up at his father. "We need a spear, your smallest spear."

Abel himself didn't keep one, but this sharp stick when brought and wielded by my younger son—I don't remember when he had had one in his hand before—proved an instrument of salvation. Feeling with his hands, he punctured the ewe's skin in just the right place, and the air emerged with such a rush that it could be heard and felt, and the animal's agony visibly turned to peace and gratitude. Abel performed the same cure on a second sheep and was bending over a third when we heard Cain's voice, "You're too slow. You're much too slow." He had his spear with him, a too-thick spear, and he began jabbing the fallen sheep at random. He didn't bend down or pretend to be careful. He stood his full squat height and moved quickly from animal to animal, deep-thrusting each one somewhere above the hind leg, both the living and the dead. Before we could stay his hand, four animals that had been breathing were dead, their wool dark with blood.

Of the precious source of meat and milk and hides, we lost eleven out of a flock of eighteen. "We must be grateful for the lucky seven," Adam declared. "We must thank the Lord. You, Abel, must offer up a firstling. And you, Cain, wild son—you must offer up the best you grow, lest the wrath of God be visited upon you."

I will never forgive myself for having remained silent over this mindless proposal that cost my son his life. It made no sense at all. Only someone besotted with the empty form of religion would have ordered such a thing. A lamb, the only one we had, was to be uselessly sacrificed, before the proper time for slaughter. We had, disastrously, plenty of meat on the ground, more than we could eat before it rotted. Our only lamb was to be slain and roasted for a God that, so far as I could see, ingested neither meat nor vegetables nor smoke nor anything else.

I didn't say a word, and my only lamb was slain.

Cain exchanged words, heated words, with his father. We were perspiring in the blazing sun—it got hotter every moment—the bloated animals at our feet and the flies already settling on them. Poor things with their woolen coats. We'd have to figure a way to get the wool off the living sheep. Do them and maybe me—I could do something with the stuff—a favor. Even the men's beards looked burdensome, though Abel's was just incipient. The idea of making fires for God, of creating more heat, seemed wildly inappropriate. All I wanted was to flee that unfortunate field and slide naked into a stream.

Tempers were naturally short, which Cain's always was anyway. I have often reflected that the weather affects our behavior. Are there places in the world with very different weather or climate and therefore very different people? We pretend that it's all free will and that we're being reasonable but sweat turns us from love and a succession of rainy days gives me cramps of body and spirit.

Cain informed his father that he was sick of his so-called revelations from heaven and all his sermonizing. A revelation to Adam, even assuming, which was doubtful, that Adam had ever had one, was not a revelation to Cain or to anyone else. He had only Adam's word for it. To Cain it was just hearsay and formed no basis for a compulsory system of religion. The apple and talking-snake story was absurd—as absurd as his mother's talking wolf and sheep—and in any case not his fault, and he was not going to pay endlessly for it. He did not take the word of his father as the word of God, which would be to put his father in the place of God. "I totally disbelieve that the Almighty ever did communicate anything to the likes of us, by any mode of speech, in any language, or by any kind of vision, or appearance, or by any means which the senses can receive. You blame me for killing the sheep but God started it. I was only doing what God did. If I should kill my brother I would be doing what God did, because God made us mortal."

Adam said over and over afterwards that *he* took that as just a bit of verbal aggression, a sally in the heat of the day, a piece of adolescent logic. Anything to score a point or win an argument, you know. The boy—or man— had been exceptionally voluble, really pouring it out.

Abel, docile, had, under his father's tuition, always gone along with the Fall story, but had avoided blaming his mother, for which I was grateful. At the Sabbath services he prayed, theed and thoud, as much as his father could wish. I remember the abrupt end of the last service, which had gone on—perfectly uselessly—the very day before. Never was there a more crushing instance of the futility of prayer.

Abel: Oh, God! Who loving, making, blessing all,
　　　Yet didst permit the Serpent to creep in
　　　And drive my father forth from Paradise,
　　　Deliver us from further evil. Hail!

Adam: Son Cain, my firstborn, wherefore art thou silent?

Cain: Why should I speak?

Adam: To pray.

Cain: Have ye not prayed?

Adam: We have, most fervently.

Cain: And loudly: I have heard you.

Adam: So will God, I trust.

Abel: Amen!

Adam: But thou, my eldest born, art silent still.

Cain: 'Tis better I should be so.

Adam: Wherefore so?

Cain: I have nought to ask.

Adam: Nor aught to thank for?

Cain: No.

Adam: Dost thou not live?

Cain: Must I not die?

Eve: Alas!

My sudden, uncontrollable weeping broke up the service.

Now, on the fatal day, two altars were constructed a few feet apart. I even cast the first stone in my blind obedience. I wanted to get it over with and go away. We gathered stones and made two circles within which the fire was to be set. Adam and Abel worked the hardest, I did a little, and Cain stood looking on, his bloody spear pointed skyward. Next the wood was piled in the rings and duly kindled. "Both blazes must be equal," said Adam, as if he were God Himself.

"But you set Abel's first, I noticed," said Cain.

"I had to set someone's first," answered his father.

The flames crackled upward, adding heat to heat. No breeze deflected them.

"You can make the first offering," added Adam. "Get your barley."

Cain stood immobile, spear planted on the ground. Their eyes met in combat. If it came to a fight! After glaring, Cain dropped his spear and went over to the edge of the field, where it was bordered by thistles and tall weeds. He pulled some of these, the juiceless, the yellow sheaf, whatever came to hand, unculled, neglected even by the grazers. With this bundle—a small one at that—he strolled over to the altar that had been designated his and flung it down.

Adam could only stare, incredulously.

The sun beat down.

"You oughtn't to have done that," Abel said.

The brothers who now looked each other in the eye, in deadly diversion of the opposition that had existed between father and son, were clad in sheepskins in grim parody of kinship, the one worn in hatred of all living creatures, the other in love and remembrance.

Abel was holding the lamb that had been groping for the teats of its dead mother. Can a dead ewe still give milk? It was hard enough for us to extract it from the living. The lamb opened wide and baaed but did not know what it had to fear, hugged and held head up like a baby.

Abel closed his eyes as Adam pierced its throat with the spear that had earlier been used for healing. My son got blood on his fuzzy chin. When it was certain that the animal was dead he flung it on the fire. The smell of singed hair ascended to heaven eddying amid the smoke. I thought of the creatures that had perished in the fire in Eden, the hippopotamus and the red fox and the deer and the chattering, panicky monkeys. We were more merciful: we killed before we burnt.

What did we expect to happen? I myself waited mindlessly, my head aching from the tension and the heat. Adam expected the Voice. Cain expected nothing, or he would not have done what he did. It was as if he had shaken his fist at the sky and challenged God to strike him dead, if He existed and could.

Abel expected approval, I'm sure, for what was for him a painful sacrifice, parental approval if not divine. The afternoon before, on the Sabbath when real work was discouraged (Adam said that God rested on the seventh day and we should too), he had brought me a handful of strawberries, just enough for one, and I had hugged him and run my fingers through his long brown tresses and then let him pop the berries into my mouth one by one. It was a trick, we both knew it, to have his fingers kissed. His father disapproved of outright kissing at the age he had reached. "Your baby is now sixteen."

So we stood there broiling and roiling, and a wind, or whirlwind, came and blew out Cain's fire, which had been smoldering anyway because of the amount of green weed and earth clumps he had thrown in it. Abel's fire flared all the more brightly towards heaven, and the delicious odor of roast lamb prevailed over the former one of burnt wool.

"The Voice has spoken," shouted Adam. "Cain, get on your knees and pray, pray for your very life. God will not be mocked."

Cain's countenance fell. You could see he inly raged. His head down, eyes on the earth to which he would return, he muttered, "What do I care about my life?" Then he lifted his head and glared at his father. By drawing himself erect to his full squat height he was showing he would never kneel and bow down.

The quarrel seemed to have reverted to one between father and son, and that was why I left. I felt Adam would be able to contain it, take care of himself, and my head was splitting. If I didn't lie down I'd faint, sunstruck (no horrible pun intended). I turned my back on them and went home.

This has occasioned centuries of remorse as I go over again and again what might have been. Abel would still be with me if I had anticipated the danger and stayed and protected him. He would never have left his mother's side as Seth did. He would have been the prop and comfort of my old age: of his father, too, the father who, also, didn't save him.

Adam made his excuses a thousand times. He pressed no commands on Cain and therefore no quarrel between them ensued. He left God to take care of Himself. The brothers walked peacefully, so far as their father could make out, into the second field, leaving the controversial altars safely behind, the stones and bones of contention. He told me he never dreamt anything would flare up between them.

I don't know that I believed him. I know that I'd have never left the two brothers alone, myself. I think Adam felt it was time to treat Abel as a man, which to him meant fully capable of self-defense if called on. Abel was already taller than his brother and if his muscles weren't bulging they should have been. I half think Adam wanted the two to fight as a test of Abel's manhood. A man is one who fights. He didn't have any other definition, such as mine: a man is one who loves.

My husband—how foolishly!—had felt it was a sufficiently good sign that Cain had left his spear where he dropped it, with the sheep's blood on it. So what could he do to Abel anyway? Punch him?

The brothers talked as they walked, and their talk got louder. Adam, who had headed for our cave, looked back. He saw Cain pick up a rock and hurl it with full force at Abel's forehead. The boy cried out, staggered, and fell, and Cain started running, running away.

I heard the cry, the last wail of the breath of life, as I lay on Abel's bed. Some instinct—also exhaustion—had put me on that bed nearer the entrance. My hands were on my aching brow. It was as if I had lifted them to protect Abel. I heard Adam's foolish preacher question as he rushed on the scene. "Where is Abel thy brother?" I heard Cain's reply, "Am I my brother's keeper?" I heard his last mockery as his voice receded in the distance. "Your God likes blood. He has it."

After the first death there is no other. Nothing can ever matter so much again.

As I stood looking at the twisted body, the cracked bone above the open eyes, the blood down the chin, a fly on the lips, one thing, one thing only, kept me erect, kept me from fainting. No, it was two things. I took command: first the body must be covered, covered with straw. Not palm leaves: dead covering, yellow-brown, dry, the barley that Cain had denied God. We pulled and trampled until nothing was left standing on the small cultivated plot that the murderer had been so conceited about. If thy eye offend thee, pluck it out, or pluck out what offends thy eye. I would have set it on fire if anything remained to offend me, just as I, afterwards, threw a brand into his cave.

After we turned our backs on the mound we both had tears in our eyes but mine burned with fury, as the thing that was in me came to expression. "Your bastard," I said. "Hunt him down. Take your spear and kill him."

Adam made a great show of bewilderment. "Bastard? What are you talking about?"

"For twenty years I have nurtured *her* child. Where is mine? Does *she* have it?"

"Eve, bereaved mother, I know how you feel on this terrible day, because your feeling is my feeling, life of my life." His tears were streaming down. "Let us get out of the sun and lie down."

I had the idea, the way he looked at me, his shining black eyes moving downward, that he was proposing to start another baby. I was to keep making them and they were to keep dying.

"Go into the forest and kill that bastard and bring me my child."

"The Lord will punish Cain. He let me know as we reaped. Cain will suffer something worse than capital punishment—life imprisonment, that is, imprisonment in life. Because the voice of his brother's blood cries from the ground, he is accursed and will be a fugitive and a vagabond in the earth, and a mark will be set on him to make sure that no one gives him the gift of death. Believe me, his punishment will be greater than he can bear."

"Did my baby die and you set beside me hers? Or does she have mine still?"

"Eve, the sun is too hot. Come."

I allowed myself to be led to my bed, where, sobbing, I turned my back on him the trickster, the trickster from whom I would never learn—no matter how much I probed—the truth of what happened to my first child. So I mourned them both, both my lost children. Lilith had my firstborn, or the earth did. Cain the murderer, the baby with the canine teeth—horrible true pun—I had dimly known from the beginning could never have come from my womb. How was it that I had passed into unconsciousness at that first birth, so conveniently for the plotters? Too conveniently. They had administered me a drug. Devils, witches—ever the drug experts. For twenty years I had sheltered a growing fiend. I had been tricked into calling him son, but he had nothing of me. No son of mine could have been what he was and done what he did. How blazingly clear it all was now!

It wasn't easy to make an individual of him, the blue-eyed baby that should have been by my side that first time. It could even have been a girl. But maybe it never opened its eyes. Maybe it was born dead, as Lilith would have wanted and perhaps willed. Adam made her pregnant at the same time and of course she needed a mother for the unwanted bastard since she would never mother anything. Or was she mothering mine, knowing from the first look how hers was and would inevitably turn out?

Lilith and Adam had my Abel's blood on them. It cried out to them from beneath the straw mound. It shrieked from the mangled bones we found the next day, after the birds and the beasts had done the carrion work that I should have foreseen but didn't. There is so much I should have foreseen.

O my son Abel, my son, my son Abel, breath of life! Would God I had died for thee, O Abel, my son, my son! As the apple tree among the trees of the wood, so is my beloved among the sons. I sat down under his shadow with great delight, and his fruit was sweet to my taste. Behold thou wert fair, my love, thou hadst doves' eyes within thy locks. Thy teeth were like a flock of sheep that came up from the washing, whereof every one bore twins. My precious lamb, lamb without blemish, and lover of lambs! Gentle—and sacrificed.

FOUR

That was the end of the altar experiment. Six days later, Sabbath again, Adam commenced a sermon on the Day of Judgment. He declared it imminent. The whole world would be burned, and we ourselves be consigned to an eternity of torture, unless we mended our ways. But I was no docile sheep to be stuffed with wind. He faltered under my gaze, and future services were confined to prayer. He left fire and thunder to the real God.

He did attempt theological argument to prove the legitimacy of Cain. He said Cain must have been conceived in Eden at our first copulation because a perfect union necessarily accomplished its purpose, conception. I retorted he was slandering all that was beautiful in that lost place. I added this was the first I heard that lovemaking had only that one purpose, and if that was true he would have a long time to wait before I let him near me, the trickster and adulterer. (I slept in Abel's bed, Adam in mine. He once made the mistake of jeering that that was what I had always wanted. He even defended his bastard by saying we didn't know what provocative words Abel had made his brother furious with.) Furthermore, I didn't see it as divinely appointed that I was to bear a child every year like a ewe. Be fruitful and multiply what—death and destruction? And why had he ever desired to mount me when I was already pregnant and therefore, by his dogma, lovemaking had no purpose? "To devilish Lilith go and do your part. Nay, I have done. You get no more of me! And I am glad, yea, glad with all my heart, that thus so cleanly I myself can free."

That was how I felt for a long while, childless and with no choice of men. The past was so bad that I wondered how I could stand the future. My life was barren.

The question of sticking to my husband agitated me day and night, as I kept him a room away but never dismissed him nor really meant him to go. What sort of marriage was it that dragged on in resentment and profound distrust? In a populous world would people leave one spouse and take another? Was the marriage bond legally dissoluble? Could you love twice? Could you even love two children? Could I ever love another child as I had loved Abel? Could I ever love another man as I had loved Adam? He *was* another man: he had become one, under a familiar, deceptive surface. And this man I found it hard to stomach.

But I kept him on. I had learned not to be certain of anything. Uncertainty is the greatest wisdom. I had digested in all its bitterness the lesson of change, sudden change. He might change. My feelings might. Nothing was permanent but change. It is presumptuous to make final decisions.

I endeavored to keep that maxim uppermost as I trembled on the edge of a cliff and looked down on the inviting waters forty feet below. All that white bubbling and eddying, that imitation of life. In infinite time, in infinite matter, in infinite space, is formed a bubble-organism, and that bubble lasts a while and bursts, and that bubble is Me. Why wait? Are we not created to be miserable and do we not all know it and invent means of deceiving each other? Here was my moment both to punish Adam and escape from myself.

I felt that something had broken within me on which my life had always rested, that I had nothing left to hold on to, and that morally my life had stopped. An invincible force—nearly invincible—impelled me to get rid of my existence, in one way or another. It cannot be said exactly that I *wished* to kill myself, for the force which drew me away from life was fuller, more powerful, more general than any mere desire. It was a force like my old aspiration to live, only it impelled me in the opposite direction. It was an aspiration of my whole being to get out of life. My state of mind was as if some wicked and stupid jest was being played upon me by someone, someone who had given me life and enabled me to give it.

Myself now the keeper of Abel's flock, I suffered sheep nightmares. I dreamt that God bade me to take my only son whom I loved and offer him up for a burnt offering upon a mountain. When we had climbed to the altar and gathered wood for it, my innocent son asked, "Behold the fire and the wood, but where is the lamb for a burnt offering?" I answered, "*You* are the lamb," and put a flint knife to his throat. And he submitted, meek as a lamb. Just before I woke up, he turned into a lamb, which was also horrible. I heard myself exclaim, "What the devil is this? He has a long snout." (I had once tried warning Cain that for every lie he told his nose would get longer. "Maybe my penis too," he said.) In another dream I cradled a sheep, thinking it was a baby. It opened its shaggy eyes and bleated.

My revulsion from sex and procreation led me to feel that Adam's advances were no better than simian. He was just a furless vertical sex-crazed monkey, with—and this was no advantage—a larger penis. I dreamt that my missing parents were black-faced gibbons. I had as much brown fur as they but they pulled it off, clumps at a time, until I was white and naked. "We are assisting," they jabbered nonsensically, "in the preservation of favored races in the struggle for life."

I didn't like our affinity with the mammals—was not mankind a creation apart?—but I noticed it more and more in my disgusted state. In construction of skull, limbs, and whole frame I saw my relatives, in brain and bone and muscle. They had points of superiority, come to think of it. It wasn't altogether fair to monkeys to compare Adam to them. I never caught the gentle, playful gibbons quarreling. I ate flesh. The monkeys ate fruit. We were killers. The gibbons were not. I had to withdraw the charge of oversexed after I witnessed two chimpanzees copulating: it was over before I could count five. That struck me as another point in their favor. None of our prolonged struggle, threshing about. Is not speed efficiency?

I realize this was a sickly attitude. Nor did it last.

For one thing, I learned, after long observation, not to think too highly of animal relationships either. I had overrated even the doves. I saw them cooing, grooming each other's feathers, and rubbing bills. How loving, I thought. How caring. Would I could be a dove, white against the sky. A bird like that could be an almost religious inspiration.

But then I discovered the male tenderness is reserved for brooding time. The husband is being temporarily kind because he wants something out of an egg. Observe him at other times: he hacks at his wife if she pauses to snap up food, drives her away from the company of others of the species, and stops harassing only when she is sitting virtuously at home in the nest. Sometimes she persuades the cock to crouch and then she mounts him and offers what I verily believe is her rear end only. Which is all he deserves.

In our fallen world the chimpanzees fought with the baboons. The blows came if stamping up and down and screeching and jabbering failed to intimidate. The chimpanzees stood upright like men to hit, kick, and bite, the very same animals who were capable with their own kind of holding hands, patting one another, embracing, and kissing. Family solidarity, I thought. Beautiful: keep outsiders away. No baboon will touch, or even look at, *my* wife. (Wrong color, anyway.) I admired the way the mother chimpanzees patiently suckled and carried around for years their increasingly heavy young. Long after the offspring started eating figs and insects they continued to claim at least a ride on mother's back.

I never dreamt that any of that tribe had any use for meat. But one day a group swung down from the branches to give black-eyed stares at a mother and her child. Would they help with the grooming, picking through the hair for nits? But the largest tore the infant from the mother's hand and dashed it on an outcrop of rock and split open the skull like a coconut. As the mother yammered, the others commenced a grisly meal.

I could have chased them with a stick, but what good would that have done? I ran away, not in fear but in disgust. We would never under any circumstances eat monkeys, whose very existence mocked us.

I would and did bite Adam in anger, but I wouldn't eat him.

As for Adam and Abel and me, if time heals all wounds it has to be said that scars are left which deaden feelings at those points. Maybe that is a protection, like wearing something hard against a weapon.

Intermittently, then permanently, I returned to Adam's bed, our bed, leaving Abel's vacant.

Would that vacancy be filled? Would the vacancy in my life be filled? Could I bear to go through another pregnancy, another bringing up? Would it prove fatal, one way or another? Had I a choice, whatever I wished? We made love—and it took, or it didn't. I lacked physiological facts. Maybe there was a season for bearing, as with birds. Maybe it depended on the phases of the moon. Maybe too many years had passed.

I had learned about growing up but not about getting weaker as an adult and aging. I had never seen an animal die of old age. They always died a violent death, like Abel. Some white hair sprouted in Adam's beard. When it proved not to be milk stain I didn't know what to make of it. "Are you tired of black?" I asked. (If he could be tired of black he could be tired of brown.) I told him it was attractive, like a variegated flower bed. He looked at my tresses but said nothing. When I discovered I myself had three white hairs I promptly pulled them out and hoped that Adam hadn't noticed. I strongly felt what was attractive in him wasn't in me.

My best hope was that if a baby came along it would be a duplicate of Abel, as monkeys were duplicates. No girl. I wanted Abel. Since Cain wasn't mine there was nothing to contradict the notion that true brothers would be very much alike, if not identical in appearance and nature. Reproduction—that was the only immortality.

So there was the stirring within me when I had nearly given up, and I bore Seth, whose name means "God has granted." He looked more like Abel than Cain—I will say that for him. But I learned there are no substitutes, even though he was a great imitator. He watched my face and changed his to have the same expression. If Adam frowned, he frowned. He copied our movements too, in turn. He was funny. He could make me laugh, and then I laughed more at his exact echo of my laughter, and if Adam was there, four voices flew around the fire, two of them his but not his. I called him Monkey, and like a monkey he reached for my sensitive places with his long thin fingers and made me giggle.

"The boy is oversexed," Adam pronounced. "He has a long penis, though thin."

"A thin boy can do the most, not having weight to hold him back."

I didn't relate to my husband an episode that took place after that six-year-old and I had bathed in the river one afternoon while Adam was napping (a habit that grew upon him as he got older). I stretched myself out naked on the grass to be dried by the sun. Seth came up to me with a finger of clay and touched my belly with it below the navel. It was quite ticklish but I lay quiet when I saw how intent he was on his work.

I looked down at what might have been a drawing of a twig (the first drawing ever), but Seth said, "Mommy, you are now a man." He then passed the back of his hand over my lower hair and sucked the moisture from the hair of the back of his hand, the way I have seen gibbons do. My monkey, my mime. He wanted to sneak up, cunning fellow, to my mouth, but I diverted him to my side. After some hugging and kissing I returned to the water and washed away my penis.

He burst into tears that I did not keep his art. He dug up blue, red, yellow, as well as white clay, with which he painted his cheeks and extended his mouth. I called him funny-face. I had to let him apply blueberries to my lips to make them redder. We both liked the touching. He said he could change the color of my hair (it was already two colors), but Adam would have none of that.

The boy refused to wash his funny-face thereafter. I suggested an alternative that would last. He should take a scraper and carve pictures in our cave, adorn our bedrooms. He showed a hand cutting a lamb. Adam called that first venture "art for meat's sake."

It was harder to praise his second carving—an elephant sticking its trunk between the rear legs of another elephant. "All mixed up about penises, I see," remarked Adam. "I hope he doesn't go on to giraffes."

"I suppose we shouldn't condemn him for his subject," I defended.

But then I was filled with consternation—and filled is the word—when he carved over my bed a human mother but a mother manifestly pregnant (a sight, of course, unknown to him) with something so enormous that it pushed her buttocks back too. Still, I had once felt like that. Seth had insight, inside-sight. But my breasts had never never come down to rest on the overhang of my belly. If a comparison is wanted, my breasts are, or were, like two young roes that are twins, which feed among the lilies.

Cain mined the earth for weapons to kill. Seth mined the earth for red ochre to color his drawings. He prepared a base of animal fat. Our cave had inflammable walls, until the smoke from the real fire darkened them. In the corner he made a red semicircle that I thought depicted the sun rising or setting. But he declared it was an eye, his eye, with eyelashes. He said it would prove to anyone that he, Seth, had done this work.

Our son, the lascivious eye, had precious little chance to catch Adam and me making love—or quarreling either. The years had weakened us for both. It was peace, yes, but less life.

As I was the first that Seth painted on, I remained the encourager of a hand that went on from finger painting to using feathers or animal-hair brushes. He even tried blowing pigment through a hollow bone. But his father indulged him as a young man—though it did not fit the Seventh-Day services—in playing with words in a way that often made no sense to me. Adam called it philosophy. It was of no use. It is no use to say, "The All hath neither Void nor Overflow." It is no use to say, "Perfection is round." Liking oranges, the only way to get to them is to change their roundness. When our son pronounced at seventeen, "Water is the stuff of which all things are made," I told him to go squeeze a rock. Though he said, "Hot is right, cold wrong," I didn't catch him thrusting his hand into the fire.

"The way up and the way down is one and the same." Advice to climbers? Take it and fall. I know. Seth monkeyed wisdom. Knowing nothing about it, he had the impudence to say, "Where there is the Tree of Knowledge, there is always Paradise."

"You say you were lied to," he added. "Suppose I were to say, 'I always tell lies.' What would you make of that?"

"A mother tries to believe her son," I smiled.

"But if my statement is true, then in making it I have shown it to be false."

"That's your trick again of words versus life. Better you painted a tortoise than playing around with 'showing' that if it had a head start on you you couldn't run and catch up, because you would have to go half the distance between you and it and half that distance and half that distance and so on. Words should be saved for something less frivolous."

Sometimes he had larger conceptions. "Symmetry is the necessity. God would not betray it. If He made Hell He would also have to have Heaven. Opposites are necessary. I draw an oval—an egg, a pregnant woman, a picture of immortality since the line never ends. Or say the oval is life and a line on the right that extends forever is eternity. Then there has to be a line on the left—preexistence. Father has neglected to mention that. I once remembered what I'm too old to remember now. Bright shoots of everlastingness. Whither is fled the visionary gleam?

"And if the soul is what moves us, there is no reason it would ever stop. It would go on somewhere else after we die, just as it had been somewhere else before we were born."

I was not the one to interrupt this sage to ask if his soul had popped out of Adam's penis. Holy, God's pun. Between the urine and the feces.

"The soul through all her being is immortal, for that which is ever in motion is immortal; but that which moves another and is moved by another, in ceasing to move ceases also to live. Only the self-moving, never-leaving self never ceases to move, and is the fountain and beginning of motion to all that moves besides. Now, the beginning is unbegotten, for that which is begotten has a beginning; but the beginning is begotten of nothing, for if it were begotten of something, then the begotten would not come from a beginning. But if unbegotten, it must also be indestructible; for if beginning were destroyed, there could be no beginning out of anything, nor anything out of a beginning; and all things must have a beginning."

He fancied if he drew a circle and a line he was proving something. Words if repeated often enough were fraught with meaning. Beginning, beginning, beginning. Rather often, to my ears, Monkey's chatter was monkey's chatter. "What am I thinking about? I am thinking about what I am thinking. And now what am I thinking about? I am thinking that I think about what I am thinking about."

He wasn't the only one who talked too much, but I'd be glad to hear anybody now.

It was long before we told Seth about Abel and Cain. I didn't particularly want him to try to paint the scene. He didn't. He talked about it as if he had never had a dead brother. "Once the relation between man and the deity is secured by sacralization of the victim, the sacrifice breaks it by destroying this same victim. Human action thus brings about a solution of continuity, and as it had previously established communication between the human reservoir and the divine reservoir, the latter will automatically fill the gap by discharging the anticipated benefit. The scheme of sacrifice consists in an irreversible operation (the destruction of the victim) with a view to setting off an equally irreversible operation on another plane (the granting of divine grace), which is required by the fact that two 'recipients,' situated at different levels, have previously been brought into communication."

"God did *not* ask for the sacrifice of Abel," replied Adam.

The next day, as we were sitting outside around the fire, Seth said, "As a painter it's hard for me to believe in what I can't see. What I can't see doesn't exist, as far as I am concerned."

"That is blasphemous," said Adam. "You can't see the wind. You can't see the aroma of the rose. Yet they exist."

"If you mean God is the wind, then say it. Am I to worship the wind that peevishly blew out Cain's offering because it wasn't meat? God the carnivore? And how do you know, by the way, that Cain did not have a just grievance against the shepherd? Abel's sheep had probably trampled on or devoured Cain's grain. What did the two say to each other? You don't know.

" 'You the favorite, goody, goddy,' " he mimed, his whole face a snarl. " 'You don't fool me and never did. You're a total fake, fake illness, fake piety, fake everything. You drove your greasy bleaters onto my living.

If I thought one drop of your blood was mine I wouldn't spill it, I'd spill my own first, but now—now, my earth shall be fertilized.' "

"You'll have a lovely future defending murderers," I commented, squirming under his insight: how did he intuit that Abel and Cain were not brothers? Had Adam rendered him a man-to-man confiding?

"I am willing to worship the moon," Seth mused. "*There* is beauty I can see. Round like a mother's breasts. A deity, a god, no—a goddess."

"The boy has sex in his head," moaned his by now sexless father, whose body age had feminized.

"Yes, the moon-goddess, where does she go when we don't see her? She goes to a cave where she keeps a beautiful youth. There and then she is making love to him. He's always there for her, asleep. He doesn't grow old and die. He just sleeps forever. A thing of beauty, a joy forever."

"The difference between that and being dead would be difficult to discriminate, not to say paint," was Adam's sarcastic retort.

"Oh, the garden of Eden has vanished, you say, but I know the lie of it still. The *lie* of it. It *is* a lie, to give me guilt. The result of sin is death. The result of sin is Seth. Why can't we just plain die, without the guilt? Animals die innocently and they don't go to hell. Anyway, one night in a woman's arms were paradise enow."

Privately I had no objection to God's turning out to be

female. But I had no reason to believe that; quite the contrary. A hand so various, or might I say contrarious?

"I shall have no trouble inventing a religion myself," Seth boasted. "A religion of the senses. Nothing can cure the soul but the senses, just as nothing can cure the senses but the soul. My religion will be without guilt, without shame, without blood, human or animal."

"Human blood is a stench to God's nostrils," Adam said. "And He never meant us to die."

"It is a pity He is so easily thwarted."

Much as he liked to proclaim, "Mind is the master of all" (to which Adam replied, "Proud son, we know by means of the mind that what it does not comprehend is more real than what it does"), the body finally prevailed over our clever son's mind. As Seth waxed in stature and in strength, it became ever plainer that he needed a woman, a wife. He had dreams that spent his seed. Not that he told me but it was I who straightened out his bed. One dream he did relate. He heard a woman's voice calling him into the forest. (I had been through that before.) When he followed the call there was a figure of light, sex uncertain. It greeted Seth with a cunning smile and began to beguile him with fair words. "O Seth, why abidest thou in a cave with a mother full of years? For it is rough, full of stones and of sand, and of trees with no good fruit on them, a wilderness without people, without future, no good place to dwell in. But all is heat or cold, weariness, and trouble."

With a flash there appeared beside the speaker a

woman in a white garment with black tresses and eyes. "Dost thou like?" came the question.

Like? Seth felt he would swoon.

"But she is the least that we have," said the demon and sprang with Seth into the air. As they passed along, there was pointed out to him a field that had been burned over, and on a charred stump was seated a she-monkey with her nose and tail destroyed, her hair singed off, her skin fissured and peeled to the quick, and all smeared with blood.

"Do you see that she-monkey? That black-tressed maiden is a she-monkey compared to the best we can offer. Come to us. Come!"

And Seth came. Seth, at seventeen, went. I lost my last child to the other side of the mountain, whoever, whatever, is there.

O where is the wanderer, the wonderer? Unrest. Youth strays. The fairest stars from heaven he required, from earth the highest raptures and the best, and all the Near and Far that he desired failed to subdue the tumult of his breast.

How old is he now?

I die alone. Neither Seth nor any son of his is coming back to bury me. That was a forlorn hope. The woods decay, the woods decay and fall; the vapors weep their burthen to the ground. Man comes and tills the field and lies above, and after many a summer dies the swan. Me only cruel immortality consumes.

The mud is dry on Adam's face. Where will I put

him? He told me that I should never leave his side, that paradise was lost because I did. It was so long ago, all that, as insubstantial as a dream. The time of goodness.

I seem to have strength now only to close my eyes. Perhaps something better will follow. There is nothing here I want to see.

Can I will to die? Can I pack mud on myself and die? Do I not have a right at last? Lord, if Thou art there, let me die. I have seen what I have seen.

I, Eve is Edward Le Comte's seventeenth book. His versatile output includes two biographies, of John Donne and a scandalous woman of Donne's time, *The Notorious Lady Essex;* the autobiographical *The Long Road Back,* a *Dictionary of Last Words;* and the novels *He and She* (1960; a finalist for the National Book Award), *The Man Who Was Afraid* (1969), and *The Professor and the Coed* (1979).

Born and educated in Manhattan, Le Comte is Professor Emeritus of English at the State University of New York at Albany. For half of his career he taught at his alma mater, Columbia University, and for three years at the University of California at Berkeley. He was honored by the Milton Society in 1985.

Edward Le Comte now lives in the Berkshires of Massachusetts with his wife, the artist Mia Münzer Le Comte, whose memoir *I Still Dream of Prague* was published in 1987. They have one son.